Alien Warriors' Obsession

M.Q. Rush

AUTHOR'S NOTE

Please Beware: This book contains explicit sexual content and is intended for adult readers only. All the characters are purely fictional and over 18 years of age. This book explores *dark* erotic themes and if you are a sensitive reader, this may not be the book for you.

(may contain spoilers ahead)
Kinks and triggers include:

Rough sex

Bondage

Dubcon

Domination and submission

Spanking

Anal play

Orgasm denial

Brief depictions of violence

Subjugation based on gender and species

These BDSM-inspired scenarios take place under purely fictional and alien circumstances, and are in no way intended to represent or guide real-life practices on planet Earth.

CONTENTS

CHAPTER 1

QUINN

The end of the world is screwing me hard, and not in a good way. Maybe today will be better.

Dust tickles my throat as I step into Estelle's ramshackle excuse for a shop. There's no such thing as retail anymore, not on Earth as it is now, but shopping at this place is like walking through the skeletal remains of the industry. It's a jungle of junk.

I've got my eye on the prize, though. I just can't let it show.

"Estelle, you old pirate." I tip an imaginary hat as I greet her. "Your prices are the only thing worse than your decor."

Hunched over the counter like some gargoyle, Estelle squints at me over her glasses, eyes narrowing beneath bushy gray brows.

"And you're as charming as a sandpaper massage, Quinn Morgyn. What're you after? Or are you just here to insult my merchandise?"

"I'm here for trade. But I could probably get better rates trading with a buzzard. At least they've got the decency to wait until you're dead before picking you clean."

"And yet here you are, sweetheart. Every week, like clockwork."

"Can't argue with that."

I feign interest in an old radio with missing knobs. Whenever I see Estelle, I have to try to get as much merchandise as possible from her. I never know when she'll pack up and leave the area, or go underground.

And who knows how long it would take to find a new vendor after that.

"I've got quality goods to trade," I tell her. "Battery packs, freshly charged. And this little beauty..." I pull out a compact solar charger, still in its original packaging, or what's left of it, anyway. It's a rare find, and I know it.

Estelle's eyes widen just a fraction—gotcha!—but she schools her features quick. "Battery packs are dime a dozen, and that charger—" she waves a dismissive hand "—probably won't last a week. I'll give you two cans of beans and a pat on the back."

"Two cans? Come on, Estelle. This thing will juice up anything from a toaster to a transport pod. We both know it's worth at least a week's rations and some clean water." I lean on her makeshift counter, arms crossed, my stance as solid as the boots I desperately want but refuse to glance at.

"Fine, fine. A week's rations. But no water. You think I'm running a charity here?"

"Throw in a bar of soap, and we've got a deal," I push, knowing full well she hoards those like gold. Cleanliness is next to godliness, especially when the world's gone to hell in a handbasket.

"Bar of soap," she echoes, mock horror painting her wrinkled features. "You drive a hard bargain."

"Someone's gotta keep things interesting around here." I flash a winning smile as I sidestep toward the pile of assorted clothing and gear. I casually inspect a faded scarf.

"Anything else catch your fancy?" Estelle grumbles, her gaze tracking my every move.

"Maybe," I murmur, letting the scarf slip through my fingers.

I catch the dull gleam of leather in my peripheral vision—the boots. They're practically singing my name, but if Estelle hears the tune, she'll have me over a barrel.

Used to be, my biggest worry was finding a pair that zipped over these thick calves of mine. Now? It's wondering if I'll have to knock over some raider's stash or get crafty with what's left of the world to keep my toes intact.

"Oh, and might as well throw in those boots over there. They look like they've seen better days, but I suppose beggars can't be choosers."

Estelle follows my casual nod. The boots are dusty, but undeniably sturdy.

"Those?" She pretends to consider, then shrugs. "Sure thing. They're a size nine, though. Might be a bit snug on you."

"Nine's close enough." I inspect my nails. Inside, I'm dancing for joy. My current boots are holding on by sheer willpower and duct tape. Thick calves be damned; I'll squeeze into those nines if it kills me.

She retrieves the boots with a grunt, placing them on the counter. My toes wiggle in anticipation. Nicely broken in, but not too shabby. They're just right, my Goldilocks dream.

Estelle eyes me, a crooked smile pulling at her lips. "Quinn, I wasn't born yesterday. You've been circling those boots like a shark since you walked in."

"Can't blame a girl for trying." I shrug, fingers itching to snatch up the boots and bolt.

"Fine," she concedes with a wave of her hand. "Take 'em. Name your price. Call this... sentimentality."

"Sentimentality?" That's a new one. Estelle's usually as sentimental as a rusted nail. I furrow my brows.

The spark in Estelle's eyes fades as she nods toward the emptier corner of the makeshift shop.

"Katarina," she murmurs. "She's gone."

I freeze, my gut clenching. I ask, even though I already know the answer: "Gone? What happened?"

"The same damn thing that's happening to all of them. The Rust Rats snatched her up last week. Sold her off to those damn Drayzok."

"Damn them," I hiss, balling my hands into fists.

Katarina, with her shy smiles and soft-spoken "thanks" whenever I helped unload stock. We weren't exactly friends, no—it's not easy to make new friends these days. But it sure was nice to see a friendly face sometimes. "She didn't deserve that... none of them do."

Estelle grunts in agreement, her mouth a tight line.

The fury boils inside me. "As if we don't have enough to worry about with the world gone to shit."

"Watch yourself out there, Quinn," Estelle warns, her eyes scanning my face. "They're getting bolder by the day."

"Let 'em try." The words come out with more bravado than I feel. I think of Katarina, too young, too gentle for the horrors of the Drayzok's touch. And here I am, still free, still fighting.

"Those Drayzok... they're like animals." The bitterness is thick in Estelle's voice.

I've heard the rumors, too. Mating in packs, in frenzies you can't stop.

They are just that, *rumors,* because there's no way to confirm what's true or not. Nobody comes back after being shipped off to be a Drayzok mate.

"Those Drayzok bastards." I shake my head.

"Yeah, and then there's talk some women go willingly." She spits on the floor. "Sick, if you ask me."

My heart trips over itself, a secret thrill at the thought. Sick? Maybe. But what does that make me, with my head filled with images of being surrounded and overpowered by the aliens? It's a dark craving that lingers at the edge of my consciousness.

I've dreamt of it before—the overpowering alien touch, the surrender. It'd be a lie to say those fantasies don't burn hot across my mind when the night gets too quiet.

It's not like it's safe to have sex with human men these days. You can't trust anyone. After having to stay on edge and alert just to survive, some small part of me thinks it might actually be nice to have someone big and strong strap me down and use me for pleasure for a while.

Not that I'd ever admit it out loud.

"Thanks for the boots," I say, shaking off my dreams.

That's all they are. Dreams. In reality, I'd fight tooth and nail before letting myself be caught.

"Watch yourself out there," Estelle warns again.

"Always do." I force a smile, clutching the boots tighter.

As I step out of Estelle's shop, the air outside tastes of dust and desperation. The sun's a real bastard today, beating mercilessly down on my neck like it's got a personal vendetta.

I kick my scooter to life. Sweat's trickling down my back, and I'm wishing for a breeze that isn't as hot as dragon breath.

As I ride, the ground's a blur beneath my wheels. Wind tugs at my hair, offering no respite from the midday inferno. Dust devils dance across the wasteland, taunting me with their carefree whirls.

I've gotta get back to shelter before the Rust Rats start prowling for flesh to sell.

But then, a flash of crude ink catches my eye. A poster, slapped onto the crumbling wall of an abandoned building. "Rewards for Captured Women" screams the headline, like we're just critters to be trapped and traded.

"Sons of bitches," I growl.

I should keep going, get back to the relative safety of my shelter. But white-hot anger propels me off the scooter. I won't let that Rust Rat filth litter the landscape unchallenged. Not today.

"Katarina, this one's for you," I whisper. I'm so damn tired of it. Of us being hunted for the Drayzok scum orbiting above.

Ten years since those solar flares turned everything on Earth to hell, and now we've got this alien freak show to contend with. It's bad enough we have to fight every day to survive this scorched rock, without our own people buying and selling us like cattle.

I hate it. Hate that we're not just scrapping against the Earth gone mad, but against those who should be our own.

I throttle down and jerk my scooter to a halt beside the obnoxious poster. The dust of the wasteland swirls around me. As I dismount, my fingers dig into the utility belt slung low on my hips, and I fish out Suzie, my homemade paintball slingshot gun.

Thanks to countless nights tweaking and perfecting her design, Suzie is precision in my hands.

I wouldn't need her if the Earth hadn't gone to shit. The solar storms set the world on fire, fried our electrical grids, and eventually led to the crumbling of our governments.

That's when the scavenger species moved in. Earth was easy prey. We didn't stand a chance, too weak to do anything about it when aliens attacked. They picked our bones clean, one raid after another, until we had almost nothing left.

Then came the Drayzok, parking their space station in Earth's orbit. They offered "protection" in exchange for our mineral resources, like lithium and water. And then, in exchange for women.

Turns out we're their favorite export.

Some protection.

With practiced ease, I load Suzie with a bright pink ball, squint one eye, aim, and let loose. The splat against the paper is satisfyingly loud. Pink streaks drip down, words blurring into an indecipherable mess.

Take that, you kidnapping scumbags.

I prowl the perimeter, Suzie cocked and loaded. Another poster, another shot—*bam*. The neon pink splashes across paper like a work of art. And another—*bam*, vivid green joining the fray.

With every defaced poster, I imagine Katarina somewhere out there, watching, knowing someone's still fighting this messed-up world for her.

But then, I hear footsteps. Grit crunches under heavy boots. I dart behind a dumpster.

Peeking out, I see them—five, maybe six Rust Rats, men looking like they've crawled out from the underbelly of hell itself. Their clothes are grimy patchworks of leather and dirt, chains clanking with every stride. Along with their trademark scars and leers, they sport piercings in places on their bodies that make me wince just thinking about it.

"Who the hell did this?" one of them growls. His beard looks like it's hosting its own ecosystem. He stares daggers at the first ruined poster.

"Fresh paint," another snarls, jabbing a dirty finger at my handiwork. "Whoever did it is still close."

He kicks at a stone, and it skitters toward my hiding place, way too close for comfort.

CHAPTER 2

QUINN

The Rust Rats prowl, wild eyes and twitching muscles. Their piercings glint in the sun, festooned with bits of metal and bone. They've got the look of men who've tasted chaos and crave more.

I press my back to the cold metal of the dumpster, biting back a curse. These guys, they're the reasons why we can't have nice things—like safety. If they lay one filthy finger on me, they'll wish they hadn't.

"Spread out!" the ringleader orders, and they fan out.

There's a rustle to my left. A shadow hovers near the dumpster's edge, and a greasy head pokes around the corner. Our eyes lock, and his widen.

"Over here!" he barks, pointing straight at me.

Damn. Time's up.

Instincts ignite. No time for fear. I leap from behind the dumpster, all adrenaline and fury. My first punch lands square on the nose of the spotter, making a satisfying crunch under my knuckle.

"Surprise," I snarl.

The others whirl around, shock flaring in their beady eyes—the kind of shock you get when the prey turns predator.

The element of surprise is my fleeting advantage. I dash forward, aiming a solid knee into the gut of the closest scumbag. A satisfying 'oomph' escapes him as he doubles over.

"Get her!"

My boot connects with another's shin, and he yelps, cursing. No time for finesse. I jab elbows, throw punches, each hit silently screaming for every woman they've ever taken. They're a blur of filthy jackets and stained teeth, but I keep moving.

Duck. Weave. Strike.

They circle me now, like a pack of predators. I'm outnumbered, but I won't go down without painting these bastards every shade of hurt.

One grabs for me, and I twist away, slamming my elbow into his nose. Blood blossoms, bright and sudden. It should scare me, being so close to losing everything. The risk should paralyze me with fear.

But it doesn't. It ignites me, burns through my veins like liquid fire.

Numbers are numbers, though, and I don't have enough on my side. They start to close in. In my mind, panic flares, along with images of cold Drayzok eyes and the horror stories of women taken.

Not going to happen to me. I'll claw out their throats first.

A lucky strike grazes my cheek. I taste iron as my lip splits. For Katarina, for all of us who refuse to be chattel, I fight harder. If they drag me to those Drayzok bastards, it'll be boots first, kicking and screaming.

They stumble, confusion in their eyes. *That's it, boys. Underestimate the fat girl. See where that gets you.*

One lunges, grabbing for my hair. Big mistake. I twist, flipping him over my hip and onto the ground. His grunt of surprise is music to my ears. Pain flares through my shoulder, but I shove it down. Can't stop, won't stop.

"Get off me!" I roar as hands claw at my jacket.

Dust kicks up around my boots as I pivot, sprinting towards the faded red beacon of my scooter. The goons are gaining ground, grunts and greedy curses filling the air behind me.

But the joke's on them. I'm not just running—I'm leading them, baiting the hook.

I reach the scooter, heart pounding a frenzied beat. They think they've got me cornered, but they don't know I've rigged this game from the start. With a practiced yank, I pull the scooter upright, swing my leg over, and feign a fumbled start.

They're almost on me, salivating at the thought of victory.

Not today, scumbags.

I kick down hard, sending the scooter into a calculated tailspin. It whirls like a dervish and crashes into the first line of Rust Rats. Bodies tumble, cries of shock slice the air, and I can't help the wild laugh that bubbles from my lips.

"Strike!" I call out. "You boys should really watch where you're going."

"Nice trick, lady," the leader sneers. He's the sort who thinks a grimy bandana is a fashion statement. The others are getting up, moaning and clutching at the body parts my scooter introduced herself to, but this guy? He doesn't flinch.

"Wasn't too bad, was it?" I shoot back, slinging my paintball gun into my hands. "You boys should take notes."

He snarls, trying to scare me. Maybe in another life, he would've. But fear is a luxury I buried alongside my parents ten years ago. Now, I'm all spitfire and survival.

He charges, armed with brute force and flailing fists. Predictable.

I sidestep, drawing Suzie in one fluid motion. Aim, breathe, fire. A splat of pink erupts across his face—the paintball's popped right into his eye.

"Argh!" he cries, hand flying to his face, paint oozing between his fingers like some grotesque tear. "My eye. You bitch!"

"Was going for a rosy complexion, but I guess pink eye works too," I quip, readying another shot.

The other Rats hesitate, watching their leader stagger and swear, pawing at his marred sight. I stand there, chest heaving, lips twisted in a half-smirk, waiting for their next move.

"Get her!" he bellows through a mouthful of curses, clutching his eye.

His pack of vermin surge forward.

These Rust Rats don't fight fair. Pain erupts across my jaw, a sucker punch from the side I didn't see coming. My legs buckle. The ground rushes up to meet me and hits my back hard enough to punch the breath from my lungs. Dust fills my mouth, grit crunching between my teeth. Boots and fists rain down.

"Thought you were tough," one of them sneers. His breath reeks of decay.

"You're gonna fetch a pretty price," another one snickers as a boot connects with my ribs.

Their laughter is cut short. Suddenly, there's a cacophony of thuds and grunts. The air shivers with something new, violence I'm not a part of.

What's this? Someone coming to my rescue? That's unheard of these days. Who would bother stopping instead of minding their own business?

Through the whirl of combat, I catch glimpses of towering forms, muscles rippling under skin that glows.

Drayzok. Here.

Someone growls, a voice deep enough to shake the earth. A Rust Rat flies over me, landing with a thud, and the others scatter, cursing.

My vision blurs, the edges of reality smudging as consciousness slips from my grasp.

I'm not being rescued. I'm being captured. And I don't even have the strength to curse my rotten luck.

The world dims, sound and fury fading into nothing.

Everything goes dark.

CHAPTER 3

QUINN

I'm slowly aware that I'm conscious.

My head's spinning, my vision's a blurry mess of colors and shapes. Groggy doesn't even begin to cover it. I blink rapidly, trying to get my bearings, but the world seems to be made out of smeared lights and shadows.

"Ugh," I groan, my voice bouncing off metal walls.

The memories hit next—flashes of fists and fury, the stench of sweat from the Rust Rats as we duked it out. But then... something else swooped in.

Oh, crap.

I've been captured by the freaking Drayzok. *Great.* The aliens. Those tech-savvy, muscle-bound brutes who think they have the right to snatch women up from our own planet.

I try to sit up, but something's holding me down. Restraints. Damn! My wrists are pinned. My legs, too. I'm spread out on a table that's way too cold against my skin, like lying on a slab of ice.

I look around. All sleek surfaces and eerie lighting, definitely not human-made. My heart hammers as I scan the room, searching for something, anything I can use to my advantage—a loose screw, a sharp edge.

But the place is spotless and sterile, like a surgery room.

Think, think, think. There's gotta be a way out. There's always a way out. Right? But everything feels too alien, too foreign. The tech looks like it's probably voice-activated or thought-controlled or whatever these extraterrestrial freaks fancy.

I twist and pull, muscles straining under the pressure, but it's no use. I'm stuck, and someone's had their fun playing dress-up with me while I was out cold.

I don't know if this counts as a dress, what I'm wearing. My curves feel all on display. It's like they've vacuum-sealed me into a single piece of fabric—one that leaves very little to the imagination.

My wounds, at least, are gone. Healed.

That's one point for alien tech, I guess.

Still, that doesn't make me feel any better about practically spilling out of this skimpy excuse for an outfit they've squeezed me into. The fabric stretches obscenely as I twist, tight in all the wrong places.

"Space creeps," I spit out. I yank at the restraints again. The table offers no give, cold under my back. The bindings tighten with every pull.

What a welcome. If this is the hospitality suite, I'd hate to see the dungeon.

A guttural garble pricks my ears. Someone's talking.

I try to make sense of it, but I don't understand a thing. Sounds like they're trying their hand at Russian, with toothpicks jammed in their throats.

A Drayzok toothpick. I can only imagine. Probably the size of a freakin' tree branch or something.

The rumble of speech comes closer as three hulking figures come into view. There's a beat of silence, and then three towering Drayzok loom over me. Looming's their thing, apparently.

The patterns on their skin are glowing like neon sin.

I'm on the verge of panic, but I force cool air through my nose. *Keep it together.*

The tallest one stalks closer.

Did I say tall? This man—beast, alien, or whatever—is massive. He's a tower of midnight blue muscle topped with horns that could skewer a buffalo. Or me, for that matter. All broad shoulders, with light patterns flickering like lightning across his skin. His eyes are narrow slits of judgment, and I swear if he had eyebrows, they'd be raised in disdain right now.

"Hi there, big guy," I say, trying to sound braver than I feel. "Love the spike action. Very... punk rock."

The spines on his back make him stand out from the other two. They quiver ever so slightly, as if tuned into some unseen tension. Under different circumstances, I'd call this guy majestic, but right now, he just looks terrifyingly in charge.

The second Drayzok is angular from head to toe, sharp lines and purple-tinted light patterns. He fiddles with some gizmo on his wrist, probably techy stuff beyond my pay grade. His jawline could cut glass, and his violet eyes are scanning me like I'm a puzzle to be solved.

He's asking me questions. I think.

"Schnak merk jow? Yinpult scarp fral'ra? Yeup schnak merk? Schnak merk? Schnak!"

"What's that mean?" I ask. "Are you the brains of this operation? Because let me tell you, buddy, abducting me? Not your brightest move."

I flex against the restraints, pretending for a second that I can give them a piece of my mind—or fist.

The alien just tilts his head, like a puzzled, oversized bird of prey.

Then there's Guy #3, the silent mountain. This third Drayzok is built like a space-faring rhino, full of bulk and brooding silence. He stands back a step, arms crossed over a chest that's all muscle and menace. His amber eyes fix on me, unblinking, like he's imagining what it would be like to snap me in half.

Or maybe he's shy?

Ha, as if.

"Got nothing to say, big guy?" I taunt, hoping to provoke some reaction.

He just grunts, and I swear the bass in his voice is so strong, the table vibrates beneath me. There's a simmering quiet about him that sets my nerves on edge. I'd bet my last paint bullet he's the sort to explode without warning. If these guys have a brute squad, he's definitely the chief enforcer.

Spike, Sharpjaw, and The Tank—nobody's offering me their names, so that's what I'm calling them in my head.

I guess I should be terrified. And part of me is, trembling beneath this skimpy fabric.

But another part, a part I'm not proud of, can't help but notice how... well, how hot they are. Damn if their alien beefcake aesthetic isn't doing something weird to my brain—or other parts.

It's like my libido's decided to throw a rave in the middle of a horror movie.

Seriously? I need to get it together.

But it's hard not to notice the way their tight uniforms outline every bulging muscle, or the exotic allure of skin that sparkles like a starry night.

It's wrong to find your captors attractive. Right? I should be thinking about how to get the hell out of here.

But escape's not exactly top of mind at the moment. Not while Spike looms over me like a personal eclipse, Sharpjaw analyzes every inch of me with that piercing gaze, and Tank exudes a silent promise of unstoppable strength. The way they ogle me, like I'm a new zoo attraction, is overwhelming.

Never thought I'd miss the Rust Rats. At least they have the decency to look guilty while double-crossing you.

But guilt's a no-show in this trio's eyes. Instead, there's something predatory and possessive.

A warning bell rings somewhere deep in my gut, instincts screaming that if someone's looking at me that way—let alone three giant someones—then I'm in danger.

But suddenly looking doesn't seem too bad, now that they've started to touch me.

The first touch is clinical. Cold, even, through the fabric of my scandalously skimpy space suit. Spike's thick fingers probe along my arms, feeling like they're long enough to wrap around twice.

These guys must be here to check me out. Maybe even to do a thorough examination before selling me off.

I wonder just how thorough they'll be.

I try to jerk away from Spike's touch, but restraints keep me from doing anything more than a pathetic wriggle.

"Hey! Watch the merchandise, you Blue Man Group reject," I bark out.

They don't seem to get it, or they don't care. Spike just tilts his horned head, light patterns pulsing in what I'm guessing is confusion. Or maybe amusement.

"Stop it!" I demand, yanking against the cold metal cuffs, but the Drayzok don't even have the decency to look sheepish.

No, if anything, they seem even more intrigued, their eyes glowing brighter as my resistance mounts.

Heat spreads on my cheeks. There's something about the way they're staring down at me like I'm the most intriguing thing they've ever seen.

This is way too close to my fantasies. But just like I knew it would be, in real life, it's way too twisted.

Sharpjaw leans in close. Too close. His eyes trace the length of my body as if he's undressing me with his gaze alone. His hands follow suit, exploring my legs, sliding up to my hips. My skin prickles under his touch, and I hate that part of me—some traitorous part—is responding to the attention.

"Stop, okay? Just—stop touching me!" My words are met with nothing more than guttural murmurs between them. It's like I'm talking to a wall.

A very large, disturbingly attractive wall.

It's silent Tank's turn, and the room's temperature seems to rise by ten degrees when he steps up. His touch is firmer, assured, as he inspects my torso.

When his hand brushes over my breast, I gasp, fighting against the squirm that wants to take over my body.

"Cut it out!" I snap, but it's like fuel to the fire for them.

Their hands become bolder. More insistent.

"Seriously, guys, personal space?" My voice climbs an octave. The shame burns, hot enough to fry an egg on my forehead.

But there's this other sensation, like bubbles of champagne fizzing through my bloodstream, and I mentally slap myself for it.

Not cool, Quinn. Not cool.

Just when I think I've hit peak mortification, Sharpjaw steps back. He raises a hand, and the others back off. For a split second, there's this flutter in my chest, a sliver of gratitude that maybe, just maybe, he's got a line he won't cross.

"Thanks. Thought you were going to—"

But the words die in my throat as he fiddles with a gizmo on his wrist, and suddenly the table shifts. Restraints pull at my limbs, and all the movement tilts me into a position that makes it crystal clear what their intentions are.

My ass is in the air. Limbs spread. I'd be glad to be off the freezing table, but now I'm exposed in the cold air, with no way to cover myself up.

"Oh, come on! What is this?"

A cold realization dawns as my legs are spread wider, the restraints tightening. The lights dim around us, leaving only the aliens' glow to illuminate the room.

I gulp. On second thought, I'm pretty sure I know exactly what this is.

These aliens aren't going to sell me. They're going to claim me as their own mate.

And they're going to do it right now.

CHAPTER 4

QUINN

I'm straining against the cold metal of the restraints, muscles screaming for release, but there's no give. Not even a millimeter.

Swearing like a sailor with a stubbed toe, I spit venom at the towering Drayzok looming over me.

"Damn you and your perversions to the deepest pit of space hell!"

I've got more curses for them where that came from. Fucking Drayzok. And damn those good-for-nothing Rust Rats back on Earth, too.

And a special "fuck you" to the Original Agents, those greedy bastards responsible for the first human contact with the Drayzok. They were the ones who sold us out, agreed to ship off women of childbearing age for mating.

Did anyone think to ask us women how we felt about this arrangement? Of course not. And now here I am, about to become Drayzok dick food.

Or something. I mean, I don't know how Drayzok dicks work, so anything's possible.

I guess I'm about to find out exactly how they work.

The aliens reach for my clothes. It doesn't take much, just a flick of one powerful wrist and all the fabric falls away, leaving me exposed.

My belly's hanging down, all floppy and unflattering, but I guess that's not a problem for Drayzok men. Their glowing eyes take in every inch of me.

Every inch. And I don't know if Drayzok men salivate, but I have a feeling those sinister mouths of theirs just got a lot wetter.

Oh hell, they're really into curves, aren't they? Spike's hands roam over my hips and belly with a reverence that should be reserved for holy things.

I feel them everywhere. Long, strong fingers trace the outline of my hips, while another pair of hands slides over my breasts, thumbs brushing nipples until they stand at attention.

Traitors.

Stop enjoying this, I tell myself, closing my eyes and biting my lip to keep from moaning. But the bite turns into a gasp when one alien twists his thick fingers over my nipple, sending shivers racing across my skin.

My eyes fly open, and I see Sharpjaw's angular features twist in fascination as he brushes a finger along my collarbone. His touch feels like a button switching something to the "on" position, igniting a primal desire within me.

"Stop it," I hiss, but it comes out weaker than I want it to.

Their skin looks alive as they touch me. Spike's patterns flicker like lightning over midnight blue. The Tank's circular swirls pulse a dark, hypnotic rhythm as he grunts.

Then Spike and The Tank each take a side, cupping my breasts with their massive hands. Heat floods my cheeks, and my nipples harden under their simultaneous touch.

Two men at once, huh? Never gone there before. But as their fingers work me over, coaxing moans from deep within my throat, the thought doesn't seem so... alien anymore.

Dammit. I'm not sure if I'm more pissed at them for doing this, or at myself for responding to their twisted game. I'm not supposed to like this.

Don't give them the satisfaction of seeing you break, I scold myself. I'm trying to arch away from them, but all I do is press myself further into their touches. I hate that it feels like heaven. It's like they're tapping directly into my nerves.

I'm already panting when suddenly Sharpjaw slides lower, pressing his hand hard against my pussy.

Now I'm gasping.

I watch the light patterns on Sharpjaw's skin. This sensation in my pussy, it's got to have something to do with those.

I stare as the glow races down his arms, across the corded muscles towards his hands.

Then the glow speeds up until it flashes its brightest—right where the heel of Sharpjaw's hand presses on my clit.

My clit explodes with sensation in response. The feeling is nothing short of *ridiculous.*

Especially because this kind of pleasure should culminate in an incredibly explosive orgasm, except Sharpjaw doesn't let me get there. He pulls away right before the orgasm hits, like he knows I was about to reach my peak and he doesn't want me to.

"Son of a..." The words trail off as I squirm, trying to chase that sensation.

But he's gone from my clit, leaving me aching.

His hands aren't enough anymore. Now he's using some sort of palm-sized device, black and sleek and humming with power.

He lets it go, and it traces lines across my torso that make my nerves sing. I've never felt anything like this before. The device slides down and hovers over my clit. My hips jerk upwards, seeking more contact.

With Spike and The Tank still fondling my breasts, it's sensory overload. Too much, yet not enough, and I'm close. So achingly close. My mind's foggy with need, and I'm almost there again, about to crest that wave—

Sharpjaw pulls the device away. Just like that. I'm left hanging, whimpering.

"You've got to be kidding me," I groan.

They don't understand the words, but they get the tone.

And they like it.

They chuckle. The sound is guttural and foreign, but it's unmistakable amusement.

"Damn you," I curse between gritted teeth.

But who am I cursing exactly? I should probably be talking to myself. I'm the one who knows just how wrong it is to enjoy their touch, but my body's reveling in it, anyway.

The worst part is that they're not letting me come. I keep getting close to an orgasm, but each time they bring me close to the edge, they yank me back, leaving me dangling precariously over a cliff of frustrated need.

I don't *want* them to make me come. It would be humiliating if they did. But dammit, if they're going to touch me like this, they could at least have the decency to let a girl get off. Every denial of release just builds the tension higher.

"God, let me finish," I beg, not caring anymore about pride or defiance.

It's all about this all-consuming need now. I'm just a mess of nerves and wants and the overwhelming desire to tip over the edge they keep me perched on.

I sag against the restraints, spent and yet not spent at all.

Maybe there's still hope of getting out of this. They haven't penetrated me yet. I've got to figure a way out before that happens.

But just as the thought forms, it's smothered under another wave of pleasure as Spike pinches my nipple.

They're still touching me, and I can't stop them. Everything I've done to keep myself safe on Earth, and nothing has prepared me for this.

When I glance at their crotches, I see giant bulges, growing bigger by the second. My gut knits into knots because deep down, I know where this is all headed.

These aliens won't be satisfied with just edging me forever. At some point, they're going to want to fuck me.

And damn it all if part of me isn't curious about what that would be like.

Three towering Drayzok males, each sporting an erection that defies what I thought I ever knew about biology.

Huge. Impossibly huge.

And now, all I can think about is what it'd be like for their enormous members to fill the void inside me. The void that their relentless teasing has carved out. I want to feel them, more than just their hands and mouths and tech-induced ecstasy.

It's not enough to be touched by these creatures.

I crave something deeper. I want it all.

And I don't even have room in my brain to be disgusted with myself for these desires anymore.

The Drayzok seem to sense my desperation, their guttural language turning into low, amused growls.

"Yes," I plead. "You know what I want. Just give it to me. Please?" My voice is hoarse, dripping with lust and frustration.

But then they stop what they're doing.

A dead halt, just like that. No warning at all. They pull their hands away, all stimulation coming to a stop, and the room goes silent except for my ragged panting.

I twist and turn, seeking any lingering touch, but there's nothing. They've backed away, their towering forms suddenly retreating as one cohesive unit.

They leave the room without a glance back, sliding the door shut with a soft hiss behind them.

"Wait!" I cry out, straining against the cold metal cuffs that hold me spread-eagle. "You can't leave me like this!"

But there's no response. Only the hollow echo of my own voice.

I can't touch myself. Can't free myself. Can't do anything but lie here, unfulfilled.

The throbbing between my legs is unbearable now, amplified by the emptiness of the room.

"Damn you, Drayzok," I choke out with a sob. "Damn you all."

CHAPTER 5

ZEGRAN

I cannot believe I'm stuck overseeing battle drills at a time like this.

The warriors under my command move with strength and discipline. Their bodies are a cascade of bioluminescent patterns beneath the harsh light of the training dome.

Usually, their grunts and shouts would be pleasing to any Drayzok warrior's ears. But today, for me, it's just noise drowning out the memory of her soft moans.

The human is back in my trio's residential unit, waiting to be claimed. My fingers twitch with the urge to ditch this place, to rush back to her. I know Thalor and Korvan are just as eager to return to her.

But according to Thalor, we're supposed to take our time before we breed her. He's read the manuals for taking a human mate, and they call this the delicate period of *fral'ra*.

Fral'ra is an important step. It involves building up your human's sexual release between periods of rest. That way, she'll become primed and ready to breed, desperate for sexual release.

It's not easy to wait when my every waking thought involves burying my cock in her soft, warm holes. My spines itch, wanting to break free from my back in a display of sexual power. I imagine her begging us for release, and dammit, I simply *cannot* believe I'm stuck overseeing battle drills at a time like this.

"More power on your thrusts!" I bark at the warriors, watching them awkwardly adjust.

They've been trying all day to impress me, but they don't realize they don't stand a chance. I will not be impressed by anything short of my human's impressive body, and that's not something my men can offer.

Scanning the ranks, I catch them stealing glances my way. Do they know? Have they heard about the human waiting in my quarters? Are they whispering among themselves about my triad's unorthodox choice?

My trio, all of us high-ranking warriors, could've had our pick of mates. Ordinarily, we would have taken our selection from the most prized human females acquired from Earth. We may have even gotten a chance to mate with a rare Drayzok female who is open to taking a male mate.

Back home on Draxith, most Drayzok males will have to go their whole lives without a mate. The discovery that human females are sexually compatible has generated great interest among us. Other Drayzok envy my trio for our high social status, which affords us our pick of mates.

It is considered highly unusual for us to spontaneously select a human mate after coming across her on the planet. But she's not just any human.

This woman is special to us.

"Keep the formation tight," I command, willing my men to focus on their drills instead of wondering about my trio's choice.

They snap to attention, addressing me with the respect due my title. "Yes, Iron Guardian Zegran!"

On the surface, I appear to be laser-focused on their movements. But my mind is on my mate.

The thought of her alone in our living space, her skin surely still flushed from our initial attempts at fral'ra, sends heat rushing through me. I recall the way her pulse quickened, how her body tensed and then shuddered.

Eager and responsive, despite her protests.

I shift uncomfortably, the battle armor feeling tighter than usual. This is maddening, this need to mark her, to resume the process and imprint on her every cell that she is ours.

I think of what I know of her so far, and how that squares with what I thought I knew about humans. When she was fighting back against those men on Earth, she didn't yield. It's an admirable trait, even among my kind.

She's fire, that one. Fight and fury. She sure seems angry with me and my trio. I don't need to understand her words to hear that she's spitting mad.

The manuals claim that it's normal for human females to show resistance this way. Just part of their usual human mating rituals. It's said that they constantly crave sexual touch, even when they pretend to protest against it.

This one is sure putting on a good show of it, though. If I didn't know any better, I'd think she truly hated us.

I wish I knew what she's been saying to us. Thalor said there's no point in fitting her with a translator chip. The manuals say her speech would be gibberish to our ears, incomprehensible due to her limited human intellect. It's a shame she won't be able to match me on an intellectual level, as a Drayzok woman could.

But she will do as a mate, regardless. Even if we cannot speak to each other, our bodies will find a shared language.

My warriors line up as we take a pause in the battle drills.

"Iron Guardian Zegran?" A young warrior speaks up. His eyes flicker back to his comrades, and with their silent encouragement, he boldly steps forward. "May I ask?"

"Speak," I command. My tone is clipped, barely concealing my impatience.

"Will our unit gain an additional slot for mating rights?" His voice quivers just slightly. "Since your triad has found an extra available human female?"

My blood goes cold. A second young warrior, mistaking my silence for permission to ask more questions, comes forward.

"We have wondered what draws your trio to this particular human," he says. "It seems that your motivation to acquire her may have been driven by your feelings, rather than your traditional right to conquer the most fertile mate?"

I can barely hear the question over the blood roaring in my ears.

This is my fault. I've been distracted today, and it seems that my young warriors have taken that as an opportunity to step out of line.

I won't repeat this mistake.

I turn to the one who asked the first question. Under my harsh gaze, the silver patterns on his skin begin to quiver.

The audacity! The suggestion that anyone else would have a claim on her, my human, sets my mind ablaze.

My spines snap to attention like blades unsheathed for war. My vision tunnels as my eyes lock onto the young warrior.

"An additional slot for mating rights?" I keep my volume low enough, but my voice booms. "You want to claim what is mine?"

His eyes widen as I draw near to him. But he holds his ground, driven by youthful recklessness. What folly!

I lunge.

My fist connects with his jaw, resounding with a crack that echoes through the training ground. He staggers back with surprise on his youthful face. Not fast enough. He should have seen this coming.

Should've known better than to covet what's mine.

"You think you're entitled to her?" Another blow, and he crumples to the metallic floor. His groans feed my flaring temper. "She is not a prize to be shared."

The spines along my back flare. My skin's bioluminescent patterns pulsate as my adrenaline surges.

He's not getting up, but I'm not letting up either. Another blow, to the gut this time, and he doubles over, gasping for breath that won't come. Not when I deliver another blow, this one to his chest.

The others recoil, distancing themselves from my rage. Good. Let them witness the consequence of overstepping.

"Your concern should be battle, not bedding!" I remind them all.

My spines retract slowly as my fury simmers.

The young warrior will need medical attention. His body is twitching on the floor. Other than that, nobody dares to move. No one is foolish enough to test me further.

Like all Drayzok warrior leaders, I am known for strict discipline. However, it has been a long time since I lost my temper to this degree with one of my charges. My acts of discipline are usually more, well, disciplined.

"Let this be a lesson to all of you," I tell the young warriors, my chest heaving. "The new human belongs to my trio. And only my trio."

My heart pounds. The urge to see her, to claim her, surges within me.

Enough of this. I'm done here. Spinning on my heel, I storm away from the drills, leaving the scent of fear and submission behind.

"Thalor. Korvan." I bark into the comm to reach the other members of my trio. "Meet me at the unit. Now."

My footsteps are hasty. The sooner we can get our human through the process of fral'ra, the better. Once we mate with her, officially claim her as our own, other males will know better than to sniff around her.

She may be resistant, but we'll make her understand. She's ours. And we will pleasure her until she's desperate for us.

CHAPTER 6

KORVAN

I stride into our residential unit, my heavy boots thumping against the metal floor. Zegran has summoned us here in the middle of the work day, but I'm sure not complaining about coming back to our human instead of finishing out my day among sweaty Drayzok men.

"Time is not in our favor," Zegran says to me and Thalor. "It's time we claim our human. Before others catch her scent."

Thalor nods vigorously, and I grunt my agreement. I'm not worried about other males, though. Like I'd let them get within spitting distance of our mate. *Not* happening.

They'd leave in pieces if they even tried to touch her.

However, if Zegran wants to hurry the process, that's up to him, as our trio's leader. I am certainly not going to argue.

So far, I may have been the most silent of us around our human, but my loins have been raging for the chance to fuck her.

"Then it's settled," I say, eager now. "We mate with her. Soon."

We enter the mating chamber, where our human is still restrained, looking exhausted. There's still fire in her dark brown eyes, though, even as she slumps against the restraints.

My gaze travels the length of her body with admiration. She is so different from the Drayzok, with her pale skin and smaller body. She is large and pillowy for her kind, but still so small compared to us.

And yet, she is clearly resilient, and I have to admire the way she's made.

Not fragile, this one. No, she's tough, and it's a turn-on.

"Is this hurting her?" Zegran asks, frowning.

"Her vital signs are stable," Thalor says. He gestures to the tech blinking at the foot of the restraint table. "The monitors track her health and remove her waste. And according to my studies, human females thrive when they focus solely on mating. It's what they want. What they need."

I snort at that. Studies or no, something tells me she's not exactly thrilled to be our little captive aphrodisiac.

But then again, what do I know about humans? Except that this one's got a fight in her that's hot enough to ignite a star.

"Let's not keep her waiting, then," I say, moving toward her.

"We have to tend to her nutritional needs first," Thalor says, skimming his fingers over packets and containers. "I've researched extensively. Zegran, give her this. It provides her hydration, with a balanced mineral content."

"Good. She looks like she could use it." Zegran lifts a water pouch to our human's lips. She gulps it down greedily, her throat working in a way that has me adjusting my pants.

"Your turn, Korvan." Thalor nudges me toward her with a nutrient bar in hand. I'm not sure if it tastes any good, but it's full of what she needs.

"Open up, sweetness," I murmur, coaxing her mouth open.

She takes it and bites hungrily. I watch her cheeks hollow with each chew.

On the last bite, she surprises me, snapping at my finger like a wildcat. Her teeth graze my skin.

"Feisty," I chuckle, shaking off the sting. The bite didn't hurt, not really, but I like the spark in her. "Looks like her energy is back. Let's prepare her for mating."

Thalor taps his wrist device and the restraints whir to life, pulling her upright until she's suspended in the air, displayed before us. Her body's splayed out now, exposed and glistening under the soft lights of the chamber.

It's a position that screams "ready," even if the scowl on her face doesn't quite match.

Zegran moves first, his fingers glowing as they come in contact with her flesh. He spreads his hands as he moves them down the human's thighs, and she closes her eyes. One might think she's trying to escape this, but the way her body is responding tells me otherwise.

I lean down to look closely at her genitals, marveling at how her folds grow pinker, puffier, and wetter. She is preparing for mating, as if her flesh was designed for this purpose.

When I reach out to touch her nipple, her eyes fly open, and she looks straight at me. I'm struck by how her nipple beads under my touch, and immediately I have to touch the other one, just to see it happen again.

Wetness glistens between her thighs, and I feel a surge of pride. We're doing something right here, no matter what her glare suggests. Yesterday's anger is still there, simmering beneath her skin, yet pleasure flickers in the depths of her eyes.

"Thalor, did the manuals mention anything about this little gem?" I gesture toward the tender nub that has become our latest obsession.

All I have to do is use the tip of my finger to lift the little hood at the top of her cunt, and already she responds with a sharp intake of breath.

"Nothing," Thalor says. "It's an interesting oversight, the fact that it's not mentioned. That thing must be packed with nerves."

"Sure looks like it," I agree. I press a knuckle into the nub and smirk when the human squirms, trying and failing to suppress a moan.

Out of the corner of my eye, I see Zegran's spines extend, a clear sign of his rising excitement.

"Her pleasure will be even more profound when she feels our cocks against it," he says.

With that image in mind, I need more. I can't help it. I slide my tongue across my lips, then dive in, bringing my mouth to her sensitive bud.

She bucks beneath me. Her throat lets out a strangled moan, and her hips grind into my face.

The more I taste her, the more I want to wreck her hole with my cock. Godsdamn, it's thrilling, watching her writhe beneath me.

So much fight in such a small package.

Her reaction is addictive. Zegran can tell I'm not eager to let up.

"Careful, Korvan," he warns. "Remember the fral'ra. We can't let her climax. Not yet."

Oh, damn it all. She tastes far too sweet to stop now, and she's almost there. Just a bit more, and I could push her over, watch her shatter into a million pieces.

I press my tongue harder against her.

"Korvan!" Zegran clamps his hand onto my shoulder, yanking me back. "Control yourself."

"Right, right," I mutter as I pull away. I suck my tongue, wanting more of her flavor.

We switch places, Zegran gliding his hands down to the human's wet folds. I watch her pink hole closely, seeing it drip as Zegran pushes his fingers inside her. She whimpers for him, and says something that sounds like pleading.

Thalor takes his turn, too. His general movements can be almost robotic at times. But here, he's smooth, working his fingers in the human's hole to make her suck in her breath before he pulls back.

We all stand back and watch the frustration surge across her face.

"Again," Zegran commands. "Bring her to the brink."

We obey. Our movements turn into choreographed chaos, tech humming, bodies pressing, mouths tasting her heated skin.

"Gods, this is better than any combat high," I groan.

This is the fral'ra—the art of breaking in a mate. And by the stars, we are artists.

I cannot stop thinking about what it'd be like to penetrate her. My body pulses with a deep, relentless need. My cock is hard as steel, aching to drive into her softness. I can feel Zegran and Thalor vibrating on the same frequency, their desires just as fierce as mine.

But she's fighting us, and Godsdamn, that makes it all the more exhilarating.

"We agreed not to take her until she's ready," Thalor reminds us, though nobody's said anything to indicate otherwise.

He senses the fiery lust among us all, and probably needs to remind himself to hold back, as well.

"What more do you need for her to be ready?" I growl, struggling to keep the beast inside me at bay. My erection feels like it's going to rip right through my clothes. "Look at her. She's soaked. Of course she's ready for us."

"True," Zegran agrees. His eyes are dark pools of lust. "But she still resists us."

As if on cue, she bucks beneath us, her glare defiant even as her body sings with need.

"Perhaps this is her way," I muse. "Maybe human females relish the fight, just as we do on the battlefield."

Her chest heaves, anger blazing in her eyes as Zegran pulls away from her cunt, once again, just before her climax.

Then, without warning, her eyes well up, and tears streak down her cheeks. She chokes, trying to hold herself back, but she can't suppress her sobs.

The sound slashes at my chest.

Dammit. This isn't the reaction we want.

"Stop," Zegran commands at once.

But he didn't need to tell us. Thalor and I have both stepped back from the human, removing our hands from her body.

"Is this... normal for humans?" I ask.

"Maybe," Thalor says, but he doesn't look so sure. He moves forward to release her from the restraints, and we watch as she crumples to the floor.

"Let's step outside," Zegran decides. We exit the chamber, leaving our mate curled up, still sobbing softly.

In the sterile light of the adjacent room, Thalor's frown cuts deep lines into his face. "Are we doing this right? Hurting her isn't our goal."

I crack my neck, rolling my shoulders. "I sort of like when she fights. It's a challenge."

Images of Drayzok females clawing at me, biting my skin in the throes of passion, flash through my mind. Drayzok females like it when we fight while we're fucking. Human women can't be that different, can they? I respect this small creature for putting up a fight.

"Are you suggesting we continue?" Zegran asks. His spines retract slightly, a sign of his uncertainty.

"I am." I know Zegran's our leader, but clearly he needs counsel. "We should discipline her. Break her. That's what she wants, isn't it? It's what we've always been told about human women."

Thalor looks troubled, his gaze flickering toward the mating chamber. "But her tears..."

I snort, remembering the aggressive Drayzok females from my past. They cried out in battle-lust, thrilled by the challenge. "Her tears are just another form of resistance. She'll come around."

"Are we sure that's the case with humans?" Thalor still hesitates, ever the thinker.

My patience wears thin. "If she's anything like a Drayzok female, she'll only respect us when we dominate her completely."

Zegran looks at Thalor. "The manuals say human women crave nonstop sex, do they not? Maybe we just need to show our mate what she wants."

"Exactly," I growl, eager to test that theory.

But Thalor still looks troubled.

"Listen," he says. "We need to understand her. Truly understand. What if we use a translator chip?"

Zegran frowns. "What about what the manuals say?"

According to the texts, a translator chip would just make a human female babble nonsense. This is due to inferior cognitive functions, supposedly.

"Regardless of the manuals," Thalor says, "I would like to give it a try. We need to figure out whether or not we're on the right track here. The chip may not work perfectly, but what if it gives us a better idea of what she's thinking?"

Zegran's spines bristle, a quiet rustle, as he mulls over the possibility. "If there's a chance this will grant us insight into her desires, then we will proceed with the translator chip."

"Alright," I concede, though my gut twists at the thought of more waiting.

If this chip doesn't work, I'm sticking with my idea. More discipline. Harder.

As we re-enter the mating chamber, our human's sweet nectar scent hits me, and anticipation quickens my pulse.

But the room is wrong. It's too quiet, the air too still. And when we look around, we see that it's vacant. No fire-eyed human glaring daggers at us.

"Frax!" The curse explodes from my lips. "She's escaped!"

"This is our own fault," Thalor says. "We were neglectful. We released her from the restraints and left the room without locking the door behind us."

"We should've known she'd get out," I agree grimly. With her sobs and tear-stained cheeks, we'd assumed she was too weak and weepy to go anywhere.

We were fools to think she'd just lie there broken. That spark in her gaze should've tipped us off.

"Find her," Zegran orders. "Before this gets out of hand."

I hope it's not too late for that.

Chapter 7

Quinn

I press my back against the cool metal wall, my nerves on high alert. The gray corridor stretches before me, illuminated by pulsing lights.

I need to get back to Earth. No freakin' clue how I'm going to make that happen, but I've taken the first step. As soon as my captors uncuffed me and stepped out of the room, I took my chance to get the hell outta there.

The circumstances are not exactly on my side here, though. I'm stark-ass naked, for one thing, and I've never been so horny in my whole damned life.

It's ridiculous, really. Here I am, sneaking through the belly of an alien spaceship, and all I can think about is how those three Drayzok hunks had me writhing.

Hell, I was tempted to masturbate as soon as they released me, to finally bring myself to the orgasm I so desperately need.

Thinking about orgasms before escape proves how damn crazy these Drayzok are making me.

No more of that. I've got to focus on escape now. Looking around, I try to move as quickly as possible away from the place those Drayzok had me in. I've got to get some distance behind me, at least, before they discover I'm missing and come after me.

With each step, I take in the dizzying scale of the corridor. It's so vast, it could swallow a dozen of my old apartment blocks whole. Every surface is slick and glossy, and bathed in a pulsing light.

There are signs overhead. I assume they offer directions, and maybe even advanced technology to transport me out of here, but I wouldn't know how to tell. The writing looks like a cross between hieroglyphs and circuit boards, making zero sense to me.

The corridor opens up into a junction, and I quickly duck behind a pillar. I risk a glance in both directions. Left or right? Eenie, meenie, miney, moe...

I hang a right. At least I'm not in the same corridor as my captors' place anymore, and that makes me feel better.

But I kinda wish I'd been able to grab some clothes on the way out. Okay, more than kinda. Cool air's hitting my exposed flesh, and I'm hyper-aware of my nakedness.

It seems silly to have to do this, but I'm grabbing my tits as I move, because I feel like my parts are slapping around loud enough to give me away.

I don't suppose there's an alien sports bra store somewhere around here?

Heavy footfalls vibrate through the metal floor, and I duck into a shadowy alcove. A pair of Drayzok warriors lumber past, their conversation a series of growls and clicks. I let out a breath, moving again as soon as they're out of sight.

I keep an eye out for hiding places as I continue, dashing into one whenever someone passes by.

One question: Where are all the women? The ship teems with Drazok males, not a single female in sight. The imbalance makes me feel even more like prey. The men are all hulking, muscular brutes, probably with more power in a single pinkie finger than I've got in my whole body. And I'm no weakling, but I know I'm no match for them.

These guys are walking tanks, giants with arms thicker than my waist and hands that could crush skulls like eggshells.

Okay. So it's a little late for this thought. But it suddenly occurs to me that I might be in more danger now than I was with my original captors.

At least there were only three of them. Who knows how many Drayzok are on this whole ship?

Who knows what they'd do to me if they saw me?

For all I know, Spike, Sharpjaw, and The Tank could be the nice ones among their kind. Maybe I don't know true Drayzok cruelty until I've met the others.

As the nearest warriors disappear from view, I dart from my hidey-hole, bare feet silent on the cold floor. I need clothes. A weapon. A plan. I need—

A blaring siren slices through the air, raising every hair on my body. Every Drayzok within view halts in place, heads swiveling. They look at each other like something important is happening. Something big.

Somehow, I have a feeling this is about me.

I crouch back down behind a pillar as a squad of Drayzok, clad in full battle gear, careens around the corner and rushes by. Their armor clinks, weapons at the ready.

Shit. I'm a naked fugitive in a spaceship full of warrior aliens who've probably already marked me as tonight's entertainment. I can't end up back in those clutches—those teasing, relentless, expert hands...

I try to dart to the next pillar, but the universe has a sick sense of humor. My foot catches on a vent and I lurch forward, arms pinwheeling. The world flips, and I'm airborne.

As I fall down to another level, the floor rushes up to meet me. I land and skid across the slick metal, momentum hurling me through an archway and into a vast, open space. I come to a hard stop on my back, the impact forcing the air from my lungs in a most ungraceful *oof*.

Fuck me sideways.

My eyes snap open to a big, wide ceiling, crisscrossed with eerie lights. I push up on my elbows, blinking.

Holy hell. This looks like a cafeteria. Tables upon tables of Drayzok men with piles of food before them. Like lunchtime at Muscle-Bound Alien Central.

Only they're not eating. The clatter of cutlery has come to a halt, and about thirty... no, more like forty pairs of glowing eyes swivel in my direction.

It's the biggest group of Drayzok I've ever seen in one place. And here I am, smack-dab in the middle of them, without a single piece of clothing to cover my bare ass. And they are all feasting on the sight of me.

Fear snakes through me, thick and icy. I think back to the stories I've heard on Earth about the Drayzok's crazed mating frenzies, triggered by the mere sight of a human woman.

Are those stories true? Either way, I'm feeling pretty fucking hopeless here. What can I possibly do against an entire hall of these testosterone-fueled giants?

Chapter 8

Quinn

The ship's alarms are a distant wail as all those pairs of Drayzok eyes burn into my skin. My heart thumps frantically. For a few long, precious seconds of stunned silence, nobody moves.

Then, chaos erupts.

All at once, the Drayzok men rise, surging at me like one big wave. I can't understand their guttural sounds, but who needs language when lust is universal? It's written all over their eager faces.

And boy, do they look eager. Their faces are twisted masks of hunger, looking to devour the unexpected feast before them. They turn their horns against each other, each trying to get ahead of the others to reach me first.

I know what they want from me. And I'm so ashamed, because just moments ago, I wanted that exact thing from my captors. I wanted them to put their cocks in me, all three of them.

But this? This is *not* what I fantasized about.

I thought Spike, Sharpjaw, and The Tank were dangerous enough, but right now, my captors look downright mild in comparison. This crowd looks much more sinister.

They swarm closer, roaring. Some of them are glowing so brightly, I have to squint my eyes just to look at them. One licks his lips as he gets closer, a lascivious gleam in his eight-foot-tall shadow. Their broad chests heave, muscles tense.

It's all teeth and tongues and too many hands reaching out for me.

They close in, and I'm an island shrinking in a sea of horny giants. I can smell the musk of anticipation coming off their dark blue skin. They're so much bigger than I am, and that fact has never been clearer than now, with every inch of my bare skin exposed to their predatory stares.

Instinct screams at me to cover up, to protect myself, but my damn useless arms are no armor against this tide.

One guy grins as he nears me, revealing sharp teeth meant more for biting than smiling. His hand darts at my arm. I scream, and he stops only because he's tackled from behind by another Drayzok.

I scramble backward, skidding my butt across the floor.

But where can I go? They're everywhere. Panic knots in my stomach, tightening as I watch them claw at me.

Is this the famed mating frenzy?

Are they about to tear me apart?

A fist slams into a jaw, and it's like the starting bell for mayhem. Drayzok warriors turn on each other, their growls rising and bouncing off metal walls.

While they keep fighting, I keep scrambling backward, ass naked on cold steel. I'm looking for a shadow to slink into, but there's nowhere to hide. I flinch as they toss each other around, because I'm painfully aware that at any second, a Drayzok warrior could go hurtling through the air and land on me, squashing me like a bug.

Then, louder than all other sounds, comes a roar that detonates all the way across the dining hall. Heads turn, and a familiar group lurches into view, fury burning on their faces.

My captors. Or, perhaps at the moment, my rescuers? Spike, Sharpjaw, and The Tank storm in, looking like the wrath of all hell.

Spike leads the charge, spines erect. His midnight blue skin throws off a glow that could shame the stars. He directs the others, and they fan out to fight.

Sharpjaw's eyes never leave mine, like he's promising from across the room not to let anyone hurt me.

No surprise, The Tank is the most brutal fighter among them. He introduces himself to the room by kicking a man's chest in and using the brutalized body to knock down several others.

Some of the other men recede. Looks like their desire for me is quenched by a sense of self-preservation that kicked in at the sight of my trio. My captors must have some rank over the rest, judging by how the once-feral crowd stands down in their presence.

But not everyone's stepping aside. Some, fueled by lust or just plain stupidity, think they still have a shot. Their patterns glow with challenge, illuminating their bulging muscles.

What a grotesque light show of stubbornness and aggression.

"All this over lil' ol' me?" I say, trying to lighten the weight of my terror even though nobody's in a joking mood.

The room becomes an arena, a battleground of lit-up skin and bellowing shouts. I watch as my captors carve their way across the room. Spike, Sharpjaw, and The Tank fight like they're making battle an art form, if you're into that sort of brutal ballet.

Which I'm not. Usually.

Muscles undulate under cobalt skin, patterns pulsating as strikes land. These guys are like walking, growling mood rings, broadcasting their fury in living color.

While Spike and Sharpjaw engage in blow-by-blow, hand-to-hand combat, The Tank just keeps tossing my would-be suitors aside like rag dolls. I'm not worried at all about whether or not he's going to get to me.

Only a little worried about what'll happen to me once he does.

I should probably be more than a "little" worried. A part of me knows I should be terrified of these three—they're my captors, after all.

But they're fighting for me, and I can't help but feel a twinge of something that might pass for gratitude.

And dammit, the sight of all their muscles flexing for me is way more arousing than it has any right to be.

The Tank, like a Greek god battering ram. Enough said.

Sharpjaw, moving in a dance of deadly grace. His lean frame slices through opponents, as if he's part machine. His eyes are still on me the whole time.

Spike is a force of nature, with his arms rippling and those lightning patterns on his skin burning with an otherworldly glow.

They're monsters, my captors. But right now, they're *my* monsters.

The last of the fighters falls. Spike looks around, as if to make sure nobody else is advancing on me.

But save for injured men writhing on the floor, nobody's moving. The fight is over.

Spike is in front of me in a couple of swift strides. Without a word, he scoops me up, one arm behind my knees, the other cradling my back. I'm airborne, hoisted against his broad chest.

We move swiftly, Sharpjaw and The Tank flanking us, forming a protective convoy as we leave the dining hall and navigate through the corridors.

Back at their quarters, the door swooshes shut behind us. My heart finally stops racing as a bubble of silence forms around us, leaving the chaos behind.

We're in their living space, but this isn't the room where they held me before. As Spike sets me down, I'm getting my first glimpse of their actual living area.

The room is all sleek lines and smooth surfaces, touches of luxury peeking through the utilitarian steel. The ceilings are tall. Plush rugs. Glowing panels casting soft shadows over sleek furniture.

It's totally different from the rest of the ship out there. This trio's got a high-status den, no doubt about it.

Sharpjaw kneels beside me. Behind him, The Tank paces like a caged beast, muscles coiled tight. They're murmuring to each other, guttural sounds that feel oddly concerned.

I think Sharpjaw's checking me for injuries, answering stern questions from Spike as he looks me over.

Spike leans in and asks me questions, too. At least, I'm pretty sure he's asking, from the way his deep voice rises at the ends of his statements.

"You know I can't understand you, right?" I say with a small laugh. But I answer what I'm pretty sure is his question anyway: "Yes, I'm okay."

Sharpjaw seems to have a different opinion. He holds a humming gadget over my skin, and tingling sensations chase away the throbbing pain from where I hit the deck. I feel oddly cared for as he heals my sore spots while Spike steadies me in place with a firm grip on my shoulders.

Okay, maybe I wasn't really okay. But I'm starting to feel better now.

That is, until the mood shifts. As soon as Sharpjaw eases the last of my soreness, he steps back and the air thickens.

The Tank grabs me, digging his fingers into my arms with a force that says he's not asking. He hauls me back to that small, stark room where this whole crazy dance began.

"Oh please, not again," I say as Sharpjaw follows, silent and solemn.

Sure enough, he shoves me back against the wall, presses a button on his wrist, and watches sternly as the restraints click over my wrists and ankles with a cold finality.

Are they pissed about the escape attempt? Is this where the "bad cop" routine kicks in? I search Sharpjaw's face for clues, but he's stoic and unreadable.

He looks at me and says something—what, I can only guess.

He might be telling me they're about to punish me for escaping.

CHAPTER 9

THALOR

I barrel down the metallic corridors of the ship, my body aching with every thunderous step. I'm sore from the brawl in the dining hall, bruises no doubt forming beneath my skin, but my wounds can wait.

I've got to get what we need and get back to our human as soon as I can. Her escape attempt was daring, yet foolish. If anything, it proves that Zegran is right: We must mate with our human as soon as possible. As long as she remains unclaimed, she is a danger to herself.

And by the stars, I would not be able to live with myself if anything bad happened to her on my watch.

Finally, I reach the tech pods, scanning the area for that elusive green-eyed maverick, Rylak. He's been dodging my attempts to contact him about snagging a translator chip for the human.

Annoyance prickles under my skin. Most Drayzok practically bow before the technician class, treating them with the reverence of demigods. Not me. I'm a warrior now, but I could have easily become a technician like Rylak. He and I have studied much of the same technology, so I see him as more of an equal than other warriors might.

I spot him tinkering with a bright green laser beam.

"Rylak!" My voice booms off the walls. "Quit dodging me. We need to talk."

"Thalor," he greets without looking up, his fingers never pausing. "You're certainly persistent."

His eyes are steady on his work, his skin patterns glowing in rigid lines.

"That's because this is important," I tell him. "I need that translator chip."

"Ah, yes. The one for your human mate?"

"You know that it is."

He finally swivels toward me, his smaller horns catching the light.

"And *you* know it's not recommended to give her a translator chip." His voice is flat, mechanical. "The brains of human females are less capable."

"I don't accept that," I snap, moving closer until I loom over him. "She needs to understand us. I want to give the chip a try."

"I can't help you." Rylak leans back, hands raised, his skin patterns growing defensive. "Drayzok authorities prohibit it. No chips for human females. Period."

"Why would they forbid it?" I frown. "It makes no sense."

"Who knows? I don't make the rules, Thalor."

"Unbelievable." I spin and leave, huffing.

It's very rare for me to consider breaking the rules the authorities set for Drayzok society. But that's exactly what I wish I could do—forget about that Godsdamned law and get my mate the translation capability she deserves.

I need to know what she's thinking, dammit. I've studied the manuals so hard, they've practically imprinted on my brain. And I know we're doing everything right, following the fral'ra to the letter.

So why is she still resisting us? Is her resistance really part of her ordinary erotic rituals, or is it a cry for help?

The translator chip would answer so many questions. I cannot accept that it's not an option.

"Thalor, did you get it?" Zegran's voice booms out before I even see him as I enter our residential unit.

I find him and Korvan sitting in the lounging area with tense postures. They rise to their feet, expectant.

"I wanted to discipline her for the escape attempt," Korvan says, his neck pulsing with restrained aggression. "Zegran made me wait."

"I decided we shouldn't do it without the chip," Zegran explains. "We need to tell her why she's being disciplined. Make sure she knows it's about her safety, staying with us."

"So where is it?" Korvan demands. "Where's the chip?"

"There is no chip," I say bitterly. "It's forbidden."

"What do you mean?" Zegran tenses.

I tell them what Rylak told me about the authorities forbidding translator chips for human females. They ask me questions—questions I, too, would like the answers to—but I have no answers for them.

"Indefensible!" Zegran's spines flare in outrage. "We can't keep waiting. If she escapes again—"

"I know," I say. "After what happened, we can't keep delaying claiming her."

Korvan snorts, cracking his neck. "Then we'll have to communicate with her the hard way. More discipline. More aggression."

His eager expression doesn't bode well for his own restraint.

"Wait." I have another option. Reaching into my utility belt, I pull out a triangular device, sleek and ominous in its simplicity.

"Another one of your tech toys?" Korvan eyes it skeptically.

"It's experimental," I warn, "but it might just kick the fral'ra into hyperdrive."

It's time to find out if it works.

CHAPTER 10

QUINN

They're back.

The door hisses open like a disgruntled cat, and my captors—Spike, Sharpjaw, and The Tank—stroll in.

Spike's the first to reach me, midnight blue muscles bulging under skin that seems to drink in the dim light. He snatches a fistful of my hair, not gentle, but not quite cruel, forcing my head up to meet his amber gaze. He grunts something low and solemn in their guttural language.

"Great pep talk," I mutter, putting on a brave front. "But your Drayzok-to-English needs work."

Spike doesn't crack a smile. Not that I've ever seen him smile. Maybe his face just doesn't do that. But he almost looks sad, like he's trying to explain something to me and he wishes I could understand.

I wish I could too, big guy.

Even though I can't make heads or tails of their guttural sounds, the earnestness in Spike's tone makes my stomach do somersaults. What is this? Are they gearing up to hurt me? Or is this the prelude to another denied climax?

I'm still trying to figure out their game. One minute they're snatching me from other Drayzok goons, fussing over my bruises like worried hens, and the next, they're handling me roughly and restraining me like their personal fuck toy.

Sharpjaw moves to my legs. He unfastens the restraints around my ankles, and for half a second, I think they might set me free. Arms next?

Nope.

My arms remain restrained, and Spike's grip on me tightens instead of loosening.

The situation only gets worse when The Tank approaches. He has an actual *whip* in his hand. It looks thick and tough and strong enough to tear through steel, let alone human flesh.

"Oh, come on!"

My eyes fall on The Tank's arms, taking in the size of his muscles. This guy could really hurt me. And it's not just his size that scares the hell out of me. It's the way he looks at me, like a challenge he's about to conquer.

"Go ahead, big man," I taunt, even as my voice shakes. I'm not going to let him break me.

But then the first strike lands. And already, I know it's going to be hell trying to withstand this pain. I can't hold back my cry as a burning sensation whips across the backs of my thighs.

The second strike follows, painting a line of fire just below the first. My muscles clench, wanting to curl away.

I can't believe they're doing this to me, when they were so concerned about my bruises from the other Drayzok. A line of pure agony blazes across my butt, seeping deep into my muscles. I bite down on a scream, while Spike just tightens his grip on my arms.

Tears spring to my eyes as I ride the wave of pain. I'd get rid of the tears if I could, but my body's reacting involuntarily as each crack splinters my resolve.

These guys nursed my wounds, and now they're marking me all on their own. There's a twisted sort of care in it that worms its way into my brain, making me almost want to yield, to submit to their every whim.

Almost.

Now Spike holds me in front of him, using just one of his massive arms to pin my back to his chest. With his other hand, his fingers trail over my breasts. The way he holds me feels like a threat, and I wish he'd touch my breasts as roughly as his hold suggests.

But instead, it's all a tease. His thumbs circle my nipples, teasing them to pebbled points that ache for more attention.

The Tank examines the welts forming on my legs and butt. He decides I've had enough for now, setting down the whip.

But then he starts touching my clit—and I'd almost rather have the whip. Because once again, he's only teasing me, dancing his fingers ever so lightly against my most sensitive flesh.

His gentleness is maddening. It's such a contradiction coming from his bulky, intimidating body.

My hips buck for more. More pressure, more anything. But the relief I crave stays agonizingly out of reach.

I'm so damned sexually frustrated, it hurts.

Sharpjaw steps into my line of sight, holding up some high-tech gizmo. It's sleek, silver, and shaped like a triangle. I eye it warily, wondering what it's for.

Some kind of fresh hell, I'm sure.

The Tank grabs my legs, gripping my thighs to force them apart. Sharpjaw leans down and applies his tech to the top of my pussy. The cool touch on my heated flesh makes me shiver.

Then it activates.

The device squeezes, tightening around my clit. I scream, and cry, and even laugh hysterically.

Because this is insanity! If I thought the teasing was bad, this is worse. So much worse.

All the sensation in my clit ramps up, like I'm heading straight to the most explosive orgasm of my life.

Only the device doesn't let me climax.

It channels all that sensation from my clit and distributes it to the rest of my body, making all of my skin feel like one big, throbbing pulse of pleasure.

My arms, my legs, and places I didn't even know could feel this good suddenly light up like erogenous zones. It's so intense, I can't stop screaming. I thrash my legs wildly.

"Please!" I yell out. "Please, please let me come. Somebody *fuck me,* goddammit!"

I am out of my mind.

"Come on, Spike," I grunt. I jut my elbow toward him, aiming for what I want most right now—that thick, hard cock tenting his pants.

But my wrists are stuck in place over my head, and I can't get nearly close enough.

Twisting my hips, I catch The Tank's eye. His eyes are black pools of hunger.

With my hands uselessly bound, my legs become my best weapon. I try to wrap them around him, squeezing as tight as I can, trying to drag him closer. To bring his cock where I need it most—inside me.

He's *so close.* I'm hurting where the whip landed on me, but I can't stop. I'm practically climbing The Tank's legs like tree trunks.

But even though he watches me with eagerness in his eyes, he makes no move to bring his cock closer. I arch my back, pushing against the air, as if I could conjure his cock through sheer willpower.

"Please!"

My eyes fall on Sharpjaw's erection, bulging in his tight black pants. My core clenches with longing. Saliva pools in my mouth, and I let it drip down my chin, no shred of dignity left to salvage.

Drooling? Please, that's the least of my concerns right now.

They're talking now, their guttural language filling the room. Are they discussing me? Their plans? I try to read their expressions, to glean some hint of their intentions.

I gulp as Spike shrugs off his shirt. The thick fabric hits the floor. The others aren't far behind him.

It's happening. They're undressing. I pull against the restraints harder, like a wild animal caught in a trap. This is it.

They're getting naked, and I can only hope that means we're all thinking the same thing: I'm ready for them.

Chapter 11

Quinn

I can't stop writhing as I look at my captors' bodies, now naked before me. The whole tableau is a beautiful sight to behold, hard muscles and glowing light patterns and all.

But let's be real, my true focus here is on those cocks.

"Jesus, Mary, and Joseph," I mutter, eyes going wide as I gawk at Spike's.

It's deep blue, veiny, and I can see it throbbing from here. Those lightning bolt patterns on his skin extend to the tip of his penis.

I remember how the patterns created pleasurable sensations from his hands when he touched me, and I have to wonder what that sensation would feel like deep inside me.

Would that huge thing even *fit* inside me?

Drayzok dicks appear to have ridges running down their lengths. I look at Sharpjaw's, dark blue and sleeker than Spike's, but no less daunting. I wonder about the extra glow on his, the nodules along the shaft. Are those some kind of technological enhancements?

Then there's The Tank's. Maybe I should've saved his nickname for his cock alone. It's thick, intimidating, and its head is a glistening bulb crowning the whole glorious thing.

Honestly, I never could've pictured a dick that thick without seeing it for myself.

My pussy clenches, so slick it's almost a joke. My inner thighs are coated. I've never been this wet before, and I know it's not all about that device on my clit. I've never been in a situation like this before either.

"Fuck," I whisper. "How is this even real?"

Sharpjaw fiddles with his wrist device, and cold metal clasps around my ankles. I'm spread wide, both my arms and legs pinned in place.

I wish I could tell them the restraints aren't necessary. I'm game.

I promise.

On second thought, as Spike comes closer with his cock in his fist, maybe they're right to restrain me. He's so big. I might just chicken out once they start to penetrate me.

But there's sure nothing I can do about it as Spike aligns himself with my entrance. He towers over me. And even if I did have a chance in hell of getting out of these restraints and past him, Sharpjaw and The Tank stand just behind him with their huge cocks in their hands.

This is it. There's no going back now.

Spike pushes the head of his monstrous cock inside me. I cry out.

My slick pussy clenches greedily to pull him in, but I know better. It's too much, the sheer size of him already stretching my slit impossibly wide.

And even though I know it seems impossible to take him, I can't stop wanting him. My clit throbs with pressure, and thanks to the alien tech clamped to it, I feel that pressure *everywhere.*

Spike pauses, his guttural voice a low rumble as he speaks to Sharpjaw.

In response, Sharpjaw presses something on his wrist, and the clamp releases my clit, the device clattering to the floor.

The damn thing has released me. *Finally* I can orgasm.

After being denied for so long, it's like a dam breaks inside me, letting a tidal wave of pleasure rush through.

My back arches off the metal, my body straining against the restraints as I come undone. My hands curl into trembling fists. My legs shake so hard, they make the metal groan around me.

I've never felt an orgasm so powerful before.

"God, yes!" I scream, not caring who hears me. Not caring about anything other than the feeling of being utterly filled up, stretched to my limits by Spike's cock.

He's all the way in me now. The spines along his back stand up, tall and proud, as he drives into me deeper, harder.

I claw at the air, wishing I had something to hold on to as he pounds into me over and over.

Spike's rhythm is unyielding, a powerhouse of raw alien strength, and I can't help but love every second of this wild ride.

"More," I gasp between ragged breaths. "Don't you dare stop."

And he doesn't. He gives me exactly what I beg for, filling me completely, claiming me in ways I didn't even know were possible.

The ridges. Oh god, the ridges.

They run up and down Spike's cock. I feel them on my inner walls, and even more as he drags himself out, almost to the tip, before plunging back inside me. It's like he's textured for my pleasure, contours raking deliciously across my clit.

The ridges don't just rub against me—they actually create a suction, building a maddening pressure right where I want it. It's a warm, pulsing caress. Almost like his cock is kissing me from the inside, coaxing my body toward another climax.

Spike's skin, once cool and almost metallic to the touch, now radiates warmth against my inner thighs. While his muscles are hard, his skin feels soft, like it's responding to my body's heat and need.

The Tank approaches, looming over us with barely restrained desire. He pushes his thick thumb between my lips. I suck on it instinctively, eyes rolling back as I taste the salty tang of his skin.

It's a show of dominance that has my insides tightening with recklessness. I'm owned, and damn if it doesn't set me ablaze with a dark thrill.

The Tank's other hand is busy, wrapped around his monstrous cock, stroking fast.

I feel myself getting wetter as I watch.

Sharpjaw joins the party, grabbing my breasts. His skin pulses against mine, the light patterns flickering. The lights intensify the sensations on my nipples until I can hardly breathe.

"Ah, fuck!" My voice breaks as another orgasm rips through me, fierce and unrelenting. I ride the wave, muscles clenching around Spike's cock while Sharpjaw's glow paints my skin with light.

They fill me up, these Drayzok men—literally, figuratively, relentlessly—and I wonder if I'll ever get enough. Whether this is punishment or paradise, I don't care. Right now, all that matters is the next thrust, the next touch, the next shattering climax.

And I'm so ready for more.

CHAPTER 12

QUINN

S pike's rhythm falters. He might not operate exactly like a human man, but I know this feeling. He's about to orgasm.

He growls—a deep, resonant sound that vibrates through my core—and then there's this flash, like a storm breaking inside him. His skin crackles with energy, metallic hues sparking as his body convulses.

I feel him shooting inside me, electricity dancing where his semen touches.

He's still glowing when he pulls out. A second later, warmth splatters across my back and belly, painting me with streaks of his semen. It feels like sparks spreading across my skin. I can't help but stare, wide-eyed and panting.

Who knew getting zapped would be such a turn-on?

I'm still dripping with Spike's semen when Sharpjaw steps up.

His cock's in hand, prepped and primed. He's always been the relatively gentle one, less grunt and snarl than the others. Maybe he'll be...

Nope. Forget gentle. Sharpjaw is full of surprises, and not the cuddly kind.

He thrusts into my pussy hard, filling the space Spike vacated. Spike's electric jizz leaks out with the new invasion. I moan and squirm under the onslaught.

Sharpjaw was the one controlling those brutal tech devices, I remember now. So no, there's no gentleness here as he grips my hips and begins to pound into me.

The patterns on his skin light up, as if he's electrified by one of his little devices. But there's nothing little about Sharpjaw's own equipment. He's *impaling* me as he fucks me.

I let out a sound that's half laughter, half scream. I'm being screwed by a creature made of stars, and I don't know whether to laugh or cry.

"Come on, then," I mutter, though I know he doesn't grasp the sass behind my words. "Do your worst."

He flashes a grin full of pointed teeth, as if he understands. I don't know if he really gets it or he's just chasing his own pleasure as he ramps up his rhythm, driving into me with the relentless force of a jackhammer. Like Spike, his ridges make suctions, and the next thing I know, my clit is exploding.

The release is seismic. I shake like a damn earthquake as I come on Sharpjaw's cock.

My vision blurs, and I'm floating, adrift in the aftershocks that ripple through me.

Then it's Sharpjaw's turn to come. He growls, deep and primal, and hotness floods me. His essence fills me up, only to spill over as he pulls free from my pussy with a sloppy, wet sound.

Like Spike did before, Sharpjaw ejaculates again, painting my skin with his heat. It's like being branded by lightning, his semen searing paths of tingling sensation across my flesh.

I feel incredible. My whole body is humming. I'm a quivering mess of post-orgasmic bliss.

I can't believe what I just endured—and craved. I didn't think I could take even one of those giant alien cocks, and I just took two in a row.

Two down...

Suddenly, I realize The Tank is looming over me. His cock is a monster, hard in his hand, and it's all for me.

Can I handle it?

I've already been stretched and filled twice over. This one could break me.

"Easy there, big guy," I mutter with chattering teeth.

My eyes stay glued to what he's packing. Is this part of my punishment, making me take such a massive cock?

The Tank says a few guttural syllables to Sharpjaw, who responds with the press of a button.

Suddenly, the restraints whir, and I'm flipped upside down, my legs splayed wide, my head pointed down. It's disorienting, gravity pulling at me in all the wrong ways.

But then again, nothing about this is right.

Blood rushes to my head, but it's nothing compared to the rush between my legs as The Tank positions himself above me.

"Shit, shit, shit," I mutter, adrenaline pumping through me.

The Tank hardly even gives me a moment to brace. He plunges in from above, his giant cock breaching me mercilessly.

A strangled cry bursts out of me.

But The Tank doesn't pause, doesn't waver. He keeps going, pounding into me with a force that's both terrifying and exhilarating.

"Fuck you for being so huge," I gasp between thrusts.

And yet, deep down, I relish the stretch. It's madness. It's carnal.

And it's not just about his size. It's also the heat from those light patterns, swirling across his skin.

The heat soothes the stretch. Somehow, it doesn't hurt like it should. It's a paradox in my pussy—a stretch that feels like a caress, a fullness that's a balm.

And it's just so relentless. I squirm, trying to shift away for a little reprieve, but Sharpjaw's quick to react. With a click, the restraints pull tighter, spreading me wider. Spike grips my hips, branding me with the strength of his fingers, holding me captive to The Tank's merciless thrusts.

God, I can't move. Can't escape.

And part of me doesn't want to.

They bark words at me, and I have no idea what they're saying, but I imagine they're commanding me to take it.

They're demanding my surrender.

And I give it to them.

I've never felt so desired before. I'm the center of their universe, and it's the most intoxicating feeling. As The Tank thrusts into me and the other two hold me in place, orgasms rip through me, one after another.

Then The Tank shudders above me, his grip tightening. His orgasm hits suddenly. Hot semen floods me and spills out, like my body can't contain his ferocity.

Then he's pulling out and painting me with it, making streaks across my belly. There's that strange warmth that buzzes like electricity, lighting up my skin.

"God, what are you doing to me?" I murmur to the three of them.

There's no answer, just the grunting and deep breathing of their satisfaction.

Lying there, a sticky, heaving mass of post-coital bliss, I can barely muster the energy to even blink. I'm sweating, the stickiness of combined fluids plastering my skin with a grotesque sheen.

I'm also panting, heaving really, with drool slipping unchecked from the corner of my mouth. Just like the slick trails of jizz oozing from between my thighs.

God, I'm a mess. But damn if I care.

"Satisfied" is an understatement.

There's some kind of perverse glee coursing through me. Am I insane? This just might mean I'm insane.

But right now, I think I'm okay with it.

"Easy," I say as Spike cradles my limp body, lifting me so Sharpjaw and The Tank can unhook me from the cold restraints.

Sharpjaw's purple eyes meet mine, a silent question there. *Am I okay?*

He wouldn't understand the words even if I tried to answer. So, instead, I nod, and that seems to be all he needs.

My head lolls against Spike's chest, his midnight blue skin now a soft haven for my weary bones. With the easy way he carries me, you'd think I was weightless, not the curvy handful I am.

We end up in what must be a spa area. It's a cavernous space. Steam swirls like spirits in the air, along with the scent of something crisp and aquatic.

We slip into a giant bath, and I have to moan at the feel of warm water licking at my aching parts.

Bubbles fizz around me, tickling my senses with their effervescence. Spike holds me while Sharpjaw's deft fingers work a lather across my skin. The soap smells foreign, yet oddly comforting, like exotic flowers.

Sharpjaw's careful ministrations soothe the tender spots along my legs, moving up my body.

The Tank pays homage to my spanked backside, his thick fingers surprisingly adept at easing the sting. I shiver as he spreads a cool cream over the reddened skin.

I'm all but boneless when they finally hoist me out of the water, droplets cascading down my curves in rivulets. There's a momentary chill before toweling arms envelop me, drying all my flesh.

Having six strong arms at work makes for a thorough job.

We move again, this time to a bedroom that feels like a sanctuary. Soft lighting and plush bedding makes it like a cocoon against the harshness outside these walls.

Spike reclines first, becoming an anchor for my spent body. His broad chest molds to my back.

From either side, Sharpjaw and The Tank join us. Their limbs tangle with mine, a triad of protection. As their warmth seeps into me, the room fades away, and so do any reservations remaining inside me.

Sure, I've got concerns. But right now, in their embrace, this is all about solace. The remnants of fear and doubt are lulled to sleep by the steady thrum of three alien hearts.

CHAPTER 13

ZEGRAN

I tower over the training grounds, spines bristling along my back. The young Drayzok warriors before me are a blur of blue limbs and clashing weapons. Beside me, Thalor's gaze flickers with that analytical light of his as he watches.

"Korvan should be here," I mutter. "The troops are not so sluggish when Korvan is watching."

"He's safeguarding our mate," Thalor says. "It's for the best. She's... unpredictable."

I grunt in agreement, the thought of our mate's fiery spirit sending an involuntary twitch through my shoulders. It's been difficult for us to leave her side, even for a second, ever since we claimed her.

Because she's addictive. But also because she's a damn flight risk.

"We locked down every exit. She won't escape again."

"Good," I tell Thalor. But there's a clawing need inside me, one that wants more than her captivity. I want her understanding. "I wish she knew it's not just about confinement. We're keeping her safe."

"Communication would solve half these issues," Thalor says.

"Damn the authorities for denying us the translator chip," I agree.

I shift my gaze across the training field, locking onto the guilty ones. They don't know I know. A few of those young jackoffs were there that day in the dining hall, going after our mate like she was their prey.

None have confessed to trying to touch what's mine. But oh, they will learn what they have done wrong.

Now that we have claimed our mate with thorough fucking, other males should be less of a problem. But whether my young subordinates admit to what they've done or not, I've already determined their punishment will be severe.

They should have known better.

"I'm sure we're following the fral'ra as the manuals instruct," Thalor says. He says it as if to reassure himself, and it's not the first time today. "Yet... it's as if she still doesn't trust us."

"Yes. I've noticed." I keep my gaze fixed on the sparring below us, but my thoughts are far from here. "She writhes beneath us, moans like she wants us. But then, she also recoils at the simplest touch, as though we might harm her."

I think of the way her eyes dart around, like she's always plotting her next escape. Not the behavior of a contented mate.

"Could it be that we misunderstood the fral'ra process?" Thalor's tech devices chime softly as he adjusts them. "Do you think that somehow we got it wrong? Should we start over?"

The idea of starting over grates in my mind. We've come this far already.

"Or maybe we just need to talk to her," Thalor says, arguing with himself. "If only we had a translator chip. She deserves to be understood, to be heard. The authorities seem to forget that humans were once capable of space travel, of complex societies. They assume the translator chip would pick up nothing but nonsense, but I wager our mate would surprise them all."

"Agreed." My fists clench tighter, knuckles popping.

I can feel Thalor's restlessness vibrating through the air between us. Suddenly, his composure shatters.

In a blur of motion, Thalor lunges forward, snatching a young warrior mid-stride. The warrior's feet dangle as Thalor hauls him up by the throat, his bioluminescent patterns flaring in a silent display of fury.

"Accuracy!" Thalor roars. He shakes the youngling, whose own patterns flicker with fear and confusion. "Your sloppy move could cost lives!"

I'm taken aback, watching the scene unfold. This isn't the Thalor I know, usually so cool and careful with his actions. This is raw, unchecked emotion pouring out of him.

This is because of our human mate. She's wormed her way under our skin, into the folds of our minds where we're weakest.

It's eating Thalor alive. And Korvan, too.

I run a hand along the spines on my back, feeling them flex instinctively. As leader, it's on me to keep us together, to fix this mess. We've got to get through to our human, make her understand that she's ours—forever.

And dammit, we need that translator chip.

Thalor releases the young warrior with a shove. The drills continue, but the energy has shifted. The remaining warriors fall back into formation with trepidation in their movements. They've seen Thalor's fury, a warning no one will dare ignore.

The Drayzok ways are etched into my spine, as much a part of me as these retractable spikes that now itch with agitation.

Orders, hierarchy, tradition. I've followed them all without question, until her.

Now, every command feels like wearing a too-tight collar, choking on doubts and what-ifs.

As I watch Thalor return to the drills, his movements controlled once more, I make the decision.

Rules be damned. My trio's harmony hinges on this, on under-standing our mate, on bridging this gap between worlds.

I stand tall, my decision firm within me. It's risky. It could unravel everything I've built, everything I am.

For the first time in my life, I'm about to break the rules.

CHAPTER 14

KORVAN

I crouch over her, the human girl, sprawled across the sleep mat. Her chest rises and falls in a rhythm that's damn near hypnotic. There's this softness to her face that gets me every time.

She looks peaceful, way different from the feisty creature who spends her waking hours being all jumpy, plotting her escapes. I don't get it—why can't she be this serene all the time?

Will she ever trust us? Is this what it'll always be like with a human mate? It's got to be exhausting for her to live this way.

The door clicks, and Zegran strides in, Thalor beside him. They join me in watching our mate sleep, three Drayzok warriors watching our human girl dream away.

The thought of her writhing beneath us, her soft body a perfect fit between our bulkier forms—it's enough to make me want to wake her up for round two... and three... however high a count she can take today.

Before my mind spirals down that pleasurable path again, Zegran tilts his head toward the exit, a clear signal. Important talk time. Splendid.

We shuffle out of the sleeping compartment, keeping our eyes on her for as long as we can. I make sure to hit the lock on the door after we exit.

In our dining alcove, I lean against cool metal, waiting for Zegran to speak. We're all wired, and I sure could use something to distract me.

But it turns out this is about our mate.

Zegran's spines bristle. "I've decided I'm going after a translator chip."

Thalor and I look at each other like our leader has grown an extra head.

"Can't do it legally," Zegran continues, "so I'm doing this on my own."

"No way," I snort.

"Yes," he says firmly. "Less risk for all of us."

"Like hell," I counter. "You'll need backup. Protection is my gig. You go, I go."

"And you'll need someone who knows the tech," Thalor adds. "I'm coming, too."

Zegran looks from me to Thalor, jaw set, weighing our words. He knows he's the leader, but he also knows we're a unit. Three parts of a well-lubricated machine.

"Fine," he finally agrees. "Let's do this."

The chill of the corridor nips at my skin as we stride through it. It's not as warm out here as it is in our residential unit, where our human mate lies in slumber.

Blissfully unaware of the chaos her very existence stirs within us.

"Tech pods are this way," Thalor says. "We'll need a technician's codes to access the chip."

We reach the tech lab, prompting the doors to slide open with a hiss.

Thalor leads us to where Rylak is hunched over a console, moving his fingers across it with a speed that screams 'busy.' His green eyes widen as we enter, the rigid patterns on his skin glowing a startled hue.

"Thalor? What brings you here?"

"Rylak, we need a translator chip," Thalor says, getting right to it.

"Again, this?" Rylak straightens up, shifting his glance between us. "I already told you, I can't authorize that for your human."

"Can't or won't?" Zegran challenges.

"Both." Rylak's back stiffens. "It's against regulations."

"Regulations be damned." My patience is wearing thin. "There has to be a way. The chip doesn't have to be logged, does it? No one would know it's for a human female."

"Korvan, you ask me to risk everything." Rylak's voice blends disbelief with disgust. "To break our society's laws for what? Your curiosity?"

"More than curiosity," I snap. "We need to understand her."

"We're not leaving without that chip, Rylak," Zegran says.

He leans closer to Rylak. There's no more room for niceties, and I can feel the shift in the air.

"We're not asking anymore," Zegran growls. "We're telling you. You will give us that chip."

Rylak's gaze flickers with conflict. But he's a technician, not a brawler. He doesn't stand a chance against the likes of us.

I step closer, letting my shadow engulf him like a dark promise. Countless battles have taught me how to move swiftly. So swiftly, he doesn't even know what's happening before I grab his wrist and pull it towards the console.

"Do it," I say, voice rumbling.

"Are you insane?" Rylak sputters.

But when my grip tightens, his resistance crumbles. He hovers his hand reluctantly over the console.

"Input your code," I command. "Now."

He moves his fingers over the console, hesitant at first and then with the resignation of one who knows the battle is lost. The light patterns on his arms flicker weakly as he dials numbers into the input panel.

The screen flashes, access granted, and the chip—a gray speck of hope—is ejected from the machine. Zegran picks it up, looking at it closely.

"Remember," Thalor says, "you didn't see us here. This never happened."

We leave the tech pod without looking back, the weight of our actions heavy in the silence between us. Zegran moves with purpose, but there's a slump to his shoulders that wasn't there before.

Shame? Perhaps. It's strange to see it on him. He's never been the kind of leader to have us break the rules before.

"What if this is all for nothing?" he mutters.

I shake my head.

"It won't be." I'm not quite as confident as I sound. "It can't be."

Chapter 15

Quinn

I blink awake, instantly aware that I'm alone on a bed.

Really? No hulking Drayzok shadow looming over me? My captors never leave me unsupervised, not since I made that break for it a few days ago.

And maybe they're right not to give me another chance to escape.

I scan for an exit. It's an automatic habit now.

There's a door that hisses loud enough to give me away, windows that don't budge, and air vents too small to fit even my pinky toe, let alone my whole fluffy body.

Not exactly the greatest of escape options.

Not to mention, my heart's not really in it this time. Finding an escape, I mean.

It's not that I've given up on getting out of here. But next time, I need a better plan. Not some half-baked 'run and hope for the best' nonsense.

For one freakin' thing, the plan should involve wearing clothes. Being chased through spaceship hallways with your bits bouncing is not an experience I recommend.

I still don't know what would've happened if those other Drayzok had gotten to me before Spike, Sharpjaw, and The Tank could rescue me. I may be their captive, but at least for the moment, being with my trio is safer than being on this space station alone.

The blanket rubs over my nipples as I shift, and I shiver a little, remembering the last time I felt such a sensation: Sharpjaw and Spike both rubbing their silky tongues over my tits.

Okay, so there's another reason I'm not exactly in a rush to leave right now. I'm kind of into it—the sex, I mean.

There's no denying the thrill that comes with these aliens' touch. They're so strong. So unpredictable. These qualities are bad news, usually, but we're not on Earth, where every day was a fight for survival. Every night, a struggle to find warmth.

Now? Well, warmth isn't an issue at all now. The Tank alone has enough body heat to power a small village. My body hums whenever my captors come near.

Speaking of which.

The door hisses, sliding open. Spike, Sharpjaw, and The Tank saunter in.

"Hey, boys," I murmur. "Back for more?"

They respond to me in their guttural language.

Grunting, Sharpjaw brushes his hand across my cheek. Spike looks down at us, his eyes burning into mine. As The Tank bends down toward me, I close my eyes, shivering with anticipation.

But they don't start touching me this time. Instead, The Tank scoops me up, and my stomach flips with a different kind of excitement.

We're going back to that room—the one with the restraints—and suddenly, I'm not sure what this is about.

"Guys?" I attempt nonchalance even though my heart's racing. "What's the game plan here?"

They don't answer, of course. The Tank sets me onto the cold, unforgiving surface of the table.

"Hey!" I protest as the metal clasps click around my wrists.

I don't like this. I mean, I don't *hate* being restrained for our sex games, but I don't know if that's what's happening here. Something feels off.

I kick out, a feeble attempt to assert some control, but The Tank just catches my ankle in one large hand and puts it into the restraints.

"Not cool, big guy," I snap.

Spike says something, and I don't know if it's meant to be a reassurance, but it doesn't make me feel any better.

"Dammit, guys," I plead as Sharpjaw secures my other ankle. "Come on, let me go!"

But I'm totally restrained now, and clearly, they have no interest in changing that.

In fact, they're making it worse. Sharpjaw presses a button, and suddenly something clamps around my head, anchoring it to the table.

This isn't kinky. This is... something else.

"Son of a—" I start, but then I see it. A needle, gleaming ominously under the sterile lights, descending from above.

I feel pressure, but not pain, as the thing inserts into the back of my neck and pulls away.

"—bitch." I finish my statement, squeezing my eyes shut.

"Interesting choice for your first word for us," a voice drawls.

I snap my eyes open. What the hell? Spike is looking down at me, his eyes shining with something that resembles amusement. The room tilts, or maybe that's just my world, spinning on its axis.

"Wait," I say to Spike. "I can understand you?"

And then he grins. Because apparently, he understands me, too.

CHAPTER 16

QUINN

My brain is fuzz.

It's taking a good, long minute to adjust to the fact that I'm hearing real words, not just guttural sounds, from the Drayzok standing before me.

"Wait, why can I understand you now?"

"We gave you a translator chip," Spike answers. "Thalor believed you may have thoughts you wish to share with us." He gestures at Sharpjaw.

"Really?" I snort. "What tipped you off—maybe the fact that I was screaming BLOODY MURDER?"

The Tank looks confused, massive shoulders bunching at his ears. "You were attempting to murder us with your screams? It was a valiant attempt, but I must tell you, it'll take more than that to eliminate a Drayzok warrior."

I could laugh. Their comical seriousness is almost endearing.

Except it's hard to forget they're dangerous aliens, especially when I'm in restraints. They've kept me captive, controlled me, made me feel things.

I can never forget what they've done to me in these restraints.

Heat pools low in my belly. The memory of pleasure is a cruel intruder, complicating my defiance. And—dammit—now I'm getting turned on.

Really? My first chance to have an actual conversation, and my mind's taking me straight back to when there was no talk, just gasping breaths and shattering climaxes.

I shake my head, trying to focus on the talking.

"Fine, so you jammed a chip in my neck to stop the screaming," I say. "But why the restraints? Afraid I'd put up too good of a fight?"

Sharpjaw steps closer. "The restraints were necessary for your own safety. We could not risk you moving during the insertion. The translation chip is delicate technology, and we did not want you harmed."

"Right, because abduction and forced mating is the pinnacle of health and safety standards." My sarcasm drips like acid, but when our gazes lock, something shimmers in his eyes. Something... regretful?

"Can you let me go now?" I ask. "Or are the shackles required for conversation?"

The three exchange looks. Then, almost reluctantly, they nod. Hands more gentle than I expect reach for the bindings at my wrists and ankles. With a series of clicks, freedom returns, blood flowing back into my numbed limbs.

It's not just relief I feel. There's also a strange kind of disappointment.

"Come," Spike says, motioning towards the door. "Let's move to a more comfortable setting."

They guide me through the maze of their functional, yet sterile, home. The place's harsh lines and cold textures give way to a room with actual cushions.

Go figure, these aliens know comfort.

I go to perch on the edge of a cushion, but the fabric is like nothing on Earth, and my butt sinks right into it. The material cradles me like a lover's hand, and I'm trying not to think about how that feels more intimate than it should.

The three Drayzok fill in around me.

"We are eager to discuss the mating process with you," Spike says.

My heart skips a beat.

"Whoa, tiger," I say, holding up a hand. "How about we start with something a little more simple? Can we exchange names, for starters? They called you Thalor, right?"

Sharpjaw nods. "Thalor Vorrek."

"I am Zegran Volkos," says Spike, the spiny-backed giant.

"Korvan Drek," grunts The Tank.

"Great," I say, injecting as much normalcy into my voice as I can muster. "I'm Quinn Morgyn."

"Quinn," Thalor repeats, rolling the sound in a way that makes it seem exotic. "It is akin to 'queen' in your tongue, yes?"

The rest of us all turn to look at him.

"You've been studying her language?" The Tank—Korvan—says.

"Someone's been doing their homework," I chuckle, impressed despite everything.

Thalor's patterns glow, and he looks flattered. "If that's what you would like to call it."

"Well, I didn't have your names before, so I had to come up with something to call you guys," I tell them. "You're Spike."

I point at Zegran, whose spines twitch in response.

"Sharpjaw for you," I gesture to Thalor, who actually looks pleased by the moniker.

"And you, big guy," I say, turning to Korvan, "are The Tank. For obvious reasons."

Laughter erupts from them. It's a laugh that vibrates through the room—and through me.

This is a nice moment, but I can't let my guard down too much. As the chuckles fade, I'm pinned under the weight of their expectant gazes.

It's not just casual conversation with these guys, I have to remind myself. I know their strength—and I know what they really want from me.

"Okay," I start, my voice more steady than I feel, "let's talk about this mating thing. You guys seem to have some... interesting ideas about sexing up human women."

Thalor perks up. "We have been informed of the custom of fral'ra among your kind."

"Excuse me?" I frown at him. "Fral'ra, what is that?"

They look at each other.

"Perhaps the word does not translate?" Thalor says. "It is the process we have been embarking on with you."

What, you mean holding me down and bringing me to the edge of an orgasm like some sadistic perverts?

I don't know why, but suddenly I'm hesitant to accuse them out loud. They seemed a lot harsher when I couldn't understand them, but still, I know they can be cruel.

"The, uh, process..." I begin. "You mean you were doing all that to me because you thought it was a human custom? Didn't you notice I was trying to resist?"

"From our understanding," Korvan says, "human females give initial resistance as part of the courtship ritual. It is said that they eventually submit to signal their acceptance of a mate."

"We were informed that human females are all open to joining with Drayzok triads," Spike says. "But first we must complete the fral'ra, the process through which our bond is solidified."

"Uh-huh. And who told you that load of crap?"

"We learned through the manuals," Thalor says. "The information comes directly from the Original Agents, the first humans from Earth who brokered the connection between our peoples."

I snort. "The Original Agents. Figures. Those sleaze bags."

Their stances stiffen.

"Is this concept of fral'ra not accurate then?" Zegran's confusion is as clear as the quiver in his spikes.

"Well, don't get me wrong, some people are really into what you guys do and how well you do it..." I lick my lips, then shake my head. Let me get back on track and not confuse these guys. "Many women might actually dig Drayzok dudes, given the chance to choose. But no one wants to be snatched up and... *fral'ra'd* without a say."

"Choose? The human women?" Thalor repeats the words as if the concept is foreign. "But how would you choose without us to guide you?"

I snort. "I'm a big girl, I can make my own decisions."

"We like that you are a big girl," Korvan says, smirking. "To us, your size is delectable—"

"Korvan. Focus," Zegran snaps. "This is not the way of true warriors."

"True warriors, huh? Is that what you guys are? Why you fought so hard for me when I escaped?"

"Quinn." I love the way Thalor says my name. "We did not know your ways. We wish to protect you, and we didn't realize you felt you needed protection *from* us."

That makes my heart squeeze, just a little. What is it about these guys that gets to me?

"There are a lot of women on Earth who feel that way," I say with a shrug. "We're pretty damn terrified of you guys."

"By the stars," Korvan murmurs, his broad shoulders slumping. "What have we done?"

Thalor lowers his eyes in shame. Zegran's spines are drooping so low, they brush against his back. And Korvan can't seem to meet my gaze at all.

"Can you forgive us?" Zegran looks sick, as if the words taste foul on his tongue. It's almost funny, seeing this giant beast of a man brought low by regret.

Are these guys really groveling at me? Part of me wants to laugh, part of me wants to rage, but there's this annoying, nagging piece of me that feels... something else. Tempted to just let it go, maybe because they look genuinely upset.

Or maybe because I'm just tired of fighting against them. What would happen if we were on the same side?

"Look, guys," I begin. "I'm not gonna lie. You scared the crap out of me. But... but maybe we can move past it."

Relief washes over their faces, comically synchronized. Good grief, they're like puppies who've just been told they're still good boys after chewing up the sofa.

"Past it," Spike echoes, nodding vigorously. His eyes glint with hope, and it's disarming.

"Again, I won't lie..." Heat creeps up my neck. "What we did, I enjoyed it. The pleasure was..." I pause, searching for the right word. "...Intense? Even the restraints, they weren't all bad."

I bite my lip as I recall the sensations. The helplessness. A rush of wetness gushes between my legs, and I shift.

"I might've even been up for it if, you know, we'd talked about it first."

"Communicated desires," Thalor murmurs. There's a hint of awe in his voice, as if I've just revealed some sacred truth.

"Exactly." My heart starts to race, whether from the confession or the proximity of their half-naked bodies, I can't tell.

All three of them shift, and I don't need to look down to know why—they're aroused, and damn, it's turning me on.

"Quinn," Zegran says, his voice deeper than before, "show us."

"Show you?" My mouth is as dry as desert sand.

"Show us how you like sex," Thalor clarifies.

"Right. Show you." Words are suddenly hard to come by, but the idea of teaching these aliens how to please me—the way I want to be pleased—has its appeal.

"Only there's something you should know," Korvan says. "About us, about Drayzok, and mating."

The others glance at him, exchanging nervous looks.

"What's that?" Is there really more to discover about them?

"Now that we have taken control and claimed you, we cannot go back from here." Korvan moves closer and inhales deeply, like he's smelling my wetness. "You've had sex with us, so you'll always trigger our need... Our need to dominate you."

Thalor nods grimly. "No matter how much you fight us."

Zegran finishes, "We will make you ours."

Now, how come that doesn't sound like bad news, exactly?

CHAPTER 17

QUINN

It's the way Zegran said it: "We will make you ours."

I swear to god, when he said "ours," the word hit me right between my legs.

There's something deeply deranged about this. I should be recoiling at their possessiveness.

Me? Owned? Never.

Never outside of a sick fantasy, anyway.

But that was back on Earth. Here, when I hear my captors claiming me, it makes me lean toward them, not away.

"Well," I say, aiming for casual despite my wobbly voice, "if we're really doing this—like, actually doing this, and not just tying me up and calling it a day—maybe we could do it somewhere less... clinical? Not that room with all the restraints, if you don't mind."

I throw a dirty look at Korvan in particular. He looks like he'd just love to see me strapped down again.

They all glance at each other, those alien faces shifting in subtle ways I'm just starting to figure out.

"The mating chamber," Thalor says. "It is designed for optimal pleasure extraction."

I can't help it—I snort. "That's your problem right there. You make everything sound like a science experiment. Ever thought about starting on a bed?"

Korvan tilts his head, his eyes all bright and wired. "Humans only enjoy sex on a bed?"

The question hits me. Suddenly my brain is full of images.

Hot, filthy images.

Me, bent over their kitchen counter, Zegran's huge body pressed up behind me. Korvan hauling me into their monster-sized bathing pool, water sloshing everywhere as he manhandles me onto his lap. Thalor pinning me to the wall by the front door, his techy fingers lighting up my skin until my whole body's sparking.

I blink hard, cheeks burning.

"Um, no. Not just beds." My voice comes out strangled. "Humans can do it pretty much anywhere. The floor, the shower, against walls, in vehicles... creativity isn't exactly our problem."

They stare at me, all three of them. I try not to squirm. It doesn't really work.

"But," I continue, trying to regain some composure, "a bed is traditional. Comfortable. It's a good place to start, especially when we're still, y'know, figuring things out between us."

"A bed," Korvan repeats, like he's making a decision.

Next thing I know, he's scooping me up. Just lifts me right off the cushion like I weigh nothing.

"Don't—" I start, the old reflex kicking in.

I want to say, *"I'm too heavy,"* like I always do when some guy tries this move. Last time a human man tried it, he almost dropped me flat on my ass.

But Korvan isn't human. He doesn't even flinch. He holds me like I'm made of feathers, not flesh and bone.

For the first time in my life, I feel small in my wide frame. Delicate, even, cradled against muscles that could crush steel.

"Your bedroom or mine?" I joke, but my voice is shaky. I don't think he notices. Or maybe he does, and he likes it.

"Mine is closest," Korvan says, already striding through the living space. Zegran and Thalor fall in behind, eyes glued to me like they're worried I'll disappear if they blink.

Korvan's room is exactly what you'd expect from a guy his size. Everything's huge: the ceiling, the furniture, especially the bed. The bed's a monster of a thing.

But there's more to it. Deep colors, glimmering metal, drapes that look expensive and alien all at once. The sheets on the bed shimmer, dark as oil.

And that's where he puts me, slow and careful, like I'm the most precious thing he's ever touched.

The material is cool under my thighs. I give the bed a little test bounce. Firm, but soft enough to sink into.

Pretty much perfect.

"So," Zegran says, standing stiffly at the foot of the bed, "how do we begin this process of having sex with you?"

That's it. I lose it. I start laughing. They're being so damn formal, like we're about to assemble furniture instead of getting intimate.

The three of them stare at me in confusion, which only makes me laugh harder.

"I'm sorry," I gasp, wiping at my eyes. "It's just—you guys make it sound like you're following an instruction manual."

"But we are attempting to understand the correct procedures," Thalor says, totally serious.

That sets me off again, and I fall back on the bed, giggling like a fool. When I finally catch my breath, I look up to see all three of them watching me with expressions ranging from puzzlement to fascination.

"Okay, first step? Relax," I say, patting the bed beside me. "Come sit. Get comfortable. This isn't a military op."

There's a pause before Zegran moves first, making the bed dip dramatically under his weight. Korvan follows, settling on my other side, while Thalor hangs back, fiddling with a tablet.

"I should record your instructions for future reference—"

"Thalor," Zegran growls. "Put that away. Be present. Not everything needs to be a scientific study."

Thalor's skin patterns flicker with what I'm starting to recognize as embarrassment, but he obediently sets the device aside and joins us on the bed.

Now I'm surrounded by them, all their heat, all their attention, pressing in. The bed barely contains all of us, and I'm hyperaware of every point where our bodies touch—Zegran's thigh against mine, Korvan's arm on my shoulder, Thalor's hand resting an inch from my own.

"So," I say, trying not to sound breathless. "Tell me about you three. How does this triad thing work, exactly? Were you assigned to each other, or did you pick?"

Zegran's spines shift slightly as he considers my question. "Drayzok males are grouped based on complementary skills and genetic markers. When we reach maturity, we undergo testing and training to prove our worthiness as potential mates."

"My technical abilities complement Zegran's leadership and Korvan's strength," Thalor explains. "We were matched as a compatible unit five cycles ago."

"So it's like arranged marriage?"

"Not exactly," Korvan says. "We compete with other trios for the right to mate. Our grouping is strategic, designed to ensure strong offspring and social stability."

"But you have to mate with three men for every woman? Why's that, are there not enough Drayzok females?"

"Correct," Zegran says, his expression darkening. "Many cycles ago, our females began to prefer each other's company over males. They became increasingly reclusive. It created... challenges in our society."

"That's why you started taking human women," I say quietly.

They go quiet for a beat. It's awkward.

"What were you doing on Earth that day?" I ask, shifting gears. "When you found me fighting those Rust Rats."

"Security assignment," Korvan says. "We were monitoring trade routes when we detected the disturbance."

I nod slowly, piecing it together. "So you would have taken any woman you found being attacked that day."

It stings a little, thinking I was just convenient. Nobody special, just a random warm body in the right place at the right time.

"No," Zegran says firmly, surprising me. His eyes lock with mine. "That is not accurate."

"We have high status among our kind," Thalor explains. "We could have selected from the most prized human females, acquired through official channels."

"But there was something about you," Korvan adds, his voice dropping. "Your fire. The way you fought those men, even outnumbered."

"Most human females we've seen cower or weep when threatened," Zegran says. "You did not. You fought back."

"We watched you before we intervened," Thalor admits. "Your resourcefulness impressed us."

I blink. This is kind of wild to hear. "You liked that I fought back?"

"We respected it," Zegran says. "Your spirit called to us. We knew then that you were meant to be ours."

Heat floods my face, and I drop my gaze. It's a strange feeling, being wanted for my strength, not despite it. My size and my fighting spirit have been survival tools, not a source of attraction. Not until now.

"Oh," I say lamely, not knowing how to respond to that.

Korvan covers my hand with his. Gentle, despite the power behind it. "You are the only mate we want, Quinn."

The way he says it makes my chest go hot and melty. I look up. They're all watching me with such intensity, it makes my breath catch.

Before I can overthink it, I reach out and touch Zegran's face, tracing his jaw. His skin is cooler than a human's, with a slight metallic quality that warms up where I touch. The light patterns pulse when my fingers glide over them.

"Show me. How do these work?" I trace a glowing pattern that runs down his neck.

"The patterns respond to emotion," Thalor explains as my fingers continue their exploration of Zegran's skin. "They intensify with arousal."

Sure enough, Zegran's patterns brighten beneath my touch, going from midnight blue to electric, glowing brighter and brighter.

"They're gorgeous," I murmur.

"They are also functional," Thalor says, his own patterns brightening. "During mating, they can transfer sensations to our partner."

I remember how their touch felt like it set my nerves on fire. "Is that why it feels so intense when you touch me?"

"Partly," Thalor says, shifting closer. "I have also integrated certain technological enhancements into my bioluminescent system."

"That device you used on me?" I ask, remembering the overload of sensations.

Pride glows in Thalor's eyes. "My own design. The device amplifies pleasure receptors and distributes sensation throughout the body."

"So you're the tech genius of the group," I say with a smile, trailing my fingers over his arm and watching the patterns follow my touch like ripples in water.

"I am proficient," he acknowledges modestly, but he's practically glowing from the praise.

My gaze shifts to Korvan, who's been watching all this with growing intensity. His patterns are swirling like crazy, circles speeding up as our eyes meet.

"And what about you?" I ask. "Any special tricks up your sleeve?"

"I am less complicated," he says, leaning in until his breath hits my lips. "But I do not know how much longer I can resist dominating you, Quinn."

God. My heart's in my throat.

"Well, there's this thing humans call foreplay," I say, pausing to swallow. "It's a way to build anticipation before the main event."

"Foreplay," Thalor repeats, like he's storing the word away. "This is similar to fral'ra?"

"No," I say firmly, meeting his gaze. "Foreplay is about mutual pleasure. It's how we prepare for penetration. Especially women, we appreciate the foreplay. All the more if we're going to take in a, uh, member as big as yours. And during foreplay, I'm allowed to orgasm. That's the main difference from fral'ra."

The three exchange looks, a silent communication passing between them.

"In that case," Zegran says, dropping his voice to a rumble that I feel in my bones, "I would very much like to make you orgasm now."

His hand slides up my thigh, and I swallow hard.

I think I'm about to experience what these aliens can really do when they're not holding back.

Chapter 18

Quinn

With Zegran's hand sliding up my thigh, my heart's thumping like an unhinged rabbit.

He leans in, his face hovering inches from mine. Those spines along his back quiver with tension, like he's barely keeping himself in check.

Then his mouth crashes into mine.

He kisses like a conqueror. No hesitation. No mercy. His lips are cold at first, but they heat up quick as they claim mine. He tastes electric, metallic and sharp with a twist of something sweet.

His hand cradles the back of my head, keeping me trapped where he wants me, tongue pushing deep and slow. He's not asking for permission.

He's taking what he wants.

When he finally pulls away, there's a burn left behind on my lips.

"Those lips are mine now," Thalor says, eyes gleaming.

Where Zegran conquered, Thalor investigates. His kiss is curious, methodical. He starts with gentle pressure, cataloging my responses as he varies the intensity.

When his teeth scrape my bottom lip, I gasp, and his light patterns spark even brighter against my cheek.

He's learning me, storing away every twitch and moan for future reference.

Thalor's tongue runs along the seam of my lips, then dips inside. He knows exactly where to touch, what to do, and it makes me melt.

He releases me with obvious reluctance, his eyes gleaming with newfound knowledge.

Korvan doesn't wait for an invitation. He just growls, grabs me, and slams his mouth into mine.

His kiss is raw hunger, all demanding pressure and devouring need. He's pure muscle, reminding me of his strength by wrapping a hand around my throat.

His tongue drives into my mouth, and he tastes wild. When he finally breaks away, we're both breathing hard, and my head is spinning.

"You taste even better than you smell," he rumbles.

I open my mouth to snap back, but they're already moving. Korvan and Thalor shift to either side, boxing me in on the bed. Zegran slides lower, settling his massive shoulders between my thighs and pushing my legs wide.

"You have no idea how enticing your scent is to us," Zegran says, his hot breath fanning across my slit. "Since the moment we found you, it's been driving me mad. So sweet. So rich."

He inhales deeply, eyes fluttering shut like he's worshipping the scent.

He can't hold back anymore. His tongue—longer and more flexible than any human's—laps at me in one broad stroke from hole to clit. I cry out, arching my back off the bed.

"Hold her," Zegran commands.

Instantly, Korvan clamps his hands down on my wrists, pinning them to the bed. Thalor copies him with my ankles, so I'm stretched out between them, completely helpless.

I should tell them it's unnecessary to hold me down. Tell them I'm not going anywhere. I want this.

Truth is, feeling the pressure of their hands and their total control over me makes me hot. My pussy clenches around nothing, growing wetter by the second.

Zegran's tongue starts slow, tracing my folds. He runs it along my labia, dips inside me, then circles my clit without quite touching it.

The teasing is maddening. I try to buck my hips, but his arms have those locked down.

"Please," I whimper, hating how needy I sound.

Zegran looks up, eyes gleaming between my thighs. "Please what?"

"My clit. Just... touch my clit."

His mouth curls into a smirk before he dips his head again. "You mean this?"

This time, he sucks my clit between his lips, and I nearly scream. After all that teasing, the direct hit is almost too much.

"Look," Thalor says. "See how his patterns are connecting with you?"

I force my eyes open. Zegran's markings are going wild, blue light streaking from his arms down his back. Where his mouth touches me, those lines seem to glow right under my skin, like I'm soaking up his energy.

"The bioluminescence carries nerve-stimulating energy," Thalor explains. "It's connecting with your nervous system, enhancing every sensation."

That explains why it feels like he's lighting me up from the inside. Every nerve in my body is on fire, nipples hard, skin prickling. Zegran licks my clit, tongue flicking fast, and my whole body pulses along with his glow.

"How do we know if you like what we're doing?" Korvan asks suddenly. "You don't have our light patterns. Tell us how to read your pleasure."

I can barely even think, let alone form words to explain.

"I could tell you," I pant. "Or I could show you. Like this."

Twisting at the waist, I wrap my thighs around Zegran's head, using the only part of my limbs I can still move freely. Pressing his face tighter against me, I grind against his mouth to show him exactly where I need his tongue.

I might be worried about suffocating the guy between these thick thighs if he were human.

But Zegran can handle it.

"Yeah," I pant. "Right there. Don't stop."

Zegran growls into me, sending vibrations all the way up my spine. His tongue moves even faster, those glowing marks burning bright, and I snap.

The orgasm hits like a bomb. I scream, body arching, as Zegran's bioluminescent energy rockets through my veins. My thighs tremble around Zegran's head and I come so hard, it feels like I might never stop.

Finally, I collapse, shaking and wrung out.

Zegran rises, mouth shiny with my arousal and eyes full of pride. Korvan and Thalor are still holding me down, gripping me tighter than before.

"You liked that," Zegran declares. It's not a question.

"Obviously," I pant, still trying to catch my breath.

"No," Thalor says, leaning in. "Not just the pleasure. The restraint. You liked being held down and forced to take it."

I look away, flushed.

"You like when we dominate you," Korvan presses in a low voice. "Admit it."

My mind flashes back to before the translation chip, when they overpowered me, teased me, kept me on the edge just to watch me squirm. When I had no voice, no choice.

"Just now was different," I whisper.

"Was it?" Zegran says. "Your body responded the same way to our fral'ra."

I hesitate, fear twisting in my gut. If I admit I like being dominated, what happens? Will they go back to treating me like before? Will they push too far, scare me, hurt me? And if they do, will they even stop when I ask them to?

"Tell us the truth," Thalor says.

"I can't," I choke out.

"You will," Korvan says, squeezing my wrist.

Tears spring to my eyes, surprising all of us. I couldn't say what the hell's going on with my emotions right now. But I give up on resisting and just answer the damn question.

"Fine! Yes, okay? I like it. I like being dominated. I like being held down. I like not having to be in control all the goddamn time."

It all spills out. "Do you know what it's like on Earth? Every second of every day is about survival. Constantly being on alert. Constantly making decisions. About who to trust, where to sleep, what's safe to eat. One wrong choice and you're dead."

My voice cracks. Fuck, I hate crying in front of people.

"When you take control, when you hold me down, I don't have to think. Don't have to carry it all. Don't have to make any decisions, because I *can't* make my own decisions. I can just... feel." A tear slides down my cheek. "And it scares me how much I need that."

Something shifts in their expressions. It's a predatory hunger mixing with something almost tender. Zegran moves first, lunging forward to capture my mouth in a bruising kiss that tastes like my own pussy.

"We will give you what you need," he promises against my lips.

I feel the change in them instantly. Their grips tighten, their postures shift. The air crackles like it's full of electricity.

"No," I snap, shoving back against Zegran's chest. I glare up. There are still tears on my cheeks, but I bare my teeth. "Not that easy. You want control? Take it from me."

I twist my wrist, breaking Korvan's hold, and Thalor lets go, too, as I scramble backward on the bed.

We're starting a game of power, of push and pull. If they want me to submit, they're gonna have to work for it.

Korvan's eyes darken, and a slow smile spreads across his face. "Gladly."

He lunges for me, but I roll away, only to smack right into Zegran, who's blocking my escape. I duck under his arm, heart pounding.

"Get over here," Thalor says, reaching for my leg again.

I kick out, connecting my foot with his chest. Not like it hurts him—he's built like a brick wall—but it buys me a second.

They box me in from three sides, herding me like prey. I fight back by twisting and clawing at them, but I never really had a shot. They're bigger, stronger, faster.

Zegran catches me around the waist, lifting me clear off the bed. I squirm in his grip, but he doesn't even blink, holding me tight while Korvan grabs my wrists, pinning them behind my back.

"Yield." Thalor closes his hand around my throat.

I bare my teeth at him, defiant to the last. "Make me."

They'll have to. And from the looks in their eyes, they're up for the challenge.

I'm pinned beneath Zegran's weight now, arms trapped behind me in Korvan's iron grip. I'm breathing hard, sweaty and slick, and I can't even pretend I'm not gushing wetness between my thighs.

Thalor stands beside the bed and grabs my jaw, tilting my face up so I can't look away.

"Open your mouth," he orders.

But it's Zegran who rises to his knees, cock out and ready, thick and blue and glowing like a space-age weapon.

I clamp my lips shut, one last stand. Korvan grabs a fistful of my hair and yanks, hard enough to make me yelp.

My mouth pops open. Zegran shoves his thumb between my lips.

"Suck," he commands.

I glare, but I close my lips around his thumb anyway, sucking obediently.

"Good girl," Zegran murmurs.

The praise sends an embarrassing thrill through me.

He pulls his thumb free and pulls his cock forward.

Up close, it's even more intimidating. Dark blue, ridged and spiraled, veined with glowing lines, thicker than anything I've ever seen. The head's bulbous, already oozing pearly fluid.

"It's too big," I protest.

But really, I want to see if he can make it fit.

"You'll take it," Zegran says, his firm voice leaving no room for argument.

He presses forward, stretching my lips so wide I can barely move my jaw.

I feel so small between them, with Zegran overpowering my mouth, Korvan gripping my head, and Thalor holding my shoulders down. I'm a big girl, and they love that about me, but compared to them, I feel downright tiny.

The first few inches fill my mouth to bursting. Zegran's ridges create a rippling sensation against my tongue. I gag when he hits the back of my throat, my jaw already aching from the stretch.

I make a muffled wailing sound, and Korvan snorts at me.

"Breathe through your nose," he says from behind me. "You'll be fine."

Then I feel him wrapping his hands around my hips and hauling my ass up.

Zegran's cock is down my throat, but now Korvan's is pressing at my pussy slit from behind, thick and hot.

"Take it," he grunts, using my wetness to slam into me with one brutal thrust.

I scream around Zegran's cock. Korvan fills me so full it hurts, but it's the best kind of pain. I'm pinned, trapped between two massive, glowing blue bodies, stretched and shaken.

They move together, Zegran pulling back as Korvan thrusts in. I'm never left empty, never alone.

Zegran's markings flash, pulsing brighter and brighter. He fists my hair, holding me in place as he fucks my face faster.

"I'm going to fill that pretty mouth," he warns, breathing raggedly.

A second later, hot liquid hits the back of my throat. It's more than a mouthful of alien cum. It's thick, almost fizzy, and it tingles all the way down. Metallic and sweet, nothing like I've ever tasted.

Zegran slides out, but he's not done. His cock pulses again, shooting glowing ribbons across my face and chest. My skin prickles with electric sparks where it lands.

Before I can even catch my breath, Thalor takes Zegran's place at my lips. His cock is not quite as thick, but it's studded with those strange techy nodules running along its length.

"Suck," he says.

I obey, my mouth still buzzing from Zegran's release.

Korvan doesn't let up behind me, pounding harder into my pussy. Each thrust rocks me forward onto Thalor's cock. My face is trapped, spit and cum dripping down my chin.

It's a degrading position, but god help me, I've never been more turned on in my life.

I notice Zegran move behind me, and then I feel his hands spreading my ass cheeks apart. Panic flares in my chest.

"Wait," I try to say, but Thalor's cock muffles me.

"We're claiming all of you," Zegran says, finger circling my puckered back entrance. "Every hole."

No way. He's too big to fuck my ass. There's just no way.

Something cool and slick drips between my cheeks. Some kind of lubricant. Zegran works one finger in, stretching me, then another. It's tight, but not awful.

It won't fit, I think, but what good does it do me to think it if Thalor won't let me speak?

Zegran lines up his cock, pressing against my tight back hole.

It hurts bad, at first. A burning stretch that causes a gurgling sound in my throat.

Thalor takes advantage of my throat opening up, shoving his cock down further.

The tight muscle of my back hole gives way, and the thick head of Zegran's cock slides in.

Slowly.

"You want more?" Zegran asks, knowing I can't answer.

He hovers in place as the others keep moving, Thalor hammering down my throat and Korvan pounding at my pussy.

Then Zegran pushes in deeper, not caring about how I scream loud enough to be heard even around Thalor's cock. Korvan chuckles, pounding my pussy harder as Zegran continues his intrusion from behind.

He pushes in deeper, until I'm stuffed to overflowing. Korvan in my pussy, Zegran in my ass, Thalor stretching out my lips.

They move together, each with bruising force, bodies working to wring every last drop of sensation from me. The glowing lines on their skin get even brighter, patterns sparking across my flesh wherever they touch. It's like fucking lightning inside of me.

I should feel degraded, used. Instead, I feel powerful. Desired. Needed.

The pressure builds, hot and unstoppable. Korvan finds my clit with his hand, pinching and rolling it.

That's all it takes. I explode, shaking so hard I can barely hold on. I come and come, lost in the pulse of their bodies and the electric glow.

My spasms trigger Thalor's release. He groans, his patterns flashing bright as hot semen fills my mouth. Like Zegran's, it buzzes on my tongue, electric and alive.

Korvan and Zegran follow almost simultaneously. Their cocks throb and their cum shoots inside me, tingling and slick, making me feel like I'm glowing from the inside.

One by one, they pull out. I feel strangely empty, but that feeling lasts only a second before I'm drawn into the sensation of them ejaculating all over my skin.

Glowing streaks light up my belly, my back, my tits.

I collapse, limp. They curl around me, giant bodies protective and warm.

"Why do you do that?" I ask in a hoarse voice when I finally catch my breath. "The... jacking off on my skin with your... stuff."

"It is how we claim a mate," Thalor explains, tracing the glowing cum on my skin with his finger. "Our ejaculate carries energy from our bioluminescent patterns. It bonds with your skin, marking you as ours."

"Other Drayzok can sense it," Korvan adds, his voice rumbling against my back. "They will know you are claimed. Protected."

"It's more than just territorial marking," Zegran says. "The energy creates a connection between us. A bond."

"So this is permanent?" I feel a twisting in my gut. "This claiming?"

"Yes," Zegran answers simply. "You are ours now. Forever."

They drift off, sleeping, wrapped around me. I lie there, staring up, watching the glow of their skin reflect on the high ceiling.

They expect me to be theirs, forever.

But I'm still planning my escape.

Okay, so maybe I'm not planning it at this *exact* moment. I'm pretty damned spent and satisfied right now—way too much to try to leave.

But eventually, I've still gotta go, right?

For some strange reason, the thought of leaving these guys, of betraying them after what we've shared... it sits like a stone in my chest.

Heavy. Painful.

I stare at their sleeping faces, so alien, yet somehow familiar now.

When did that happen? When did I stop seeing monsters and start seeing someone who might be mine?

I close my eyes, but sleep keeps its distance. All I have are questions I'm not ready to answer.

Do I want to run? Or do I want to stay?

And if I stay, what the hell does that make me?

CHAPTER 19

THALOR

I adjust the interface gloves on Quinn's hands, my fingers lingering longer than necessary. Her skin is warm, so much warmer than Drayzok flesh, and the contrast sends a pleasant shiver up my arms.

She's gotten comfortable with my touch over these past few days since we gave her the translator chip. The stiffness, the fear that used to tighten her muscles at my approach—it's gone now.

It almost feels like she trusts me. Or perhaps I'm simply more familiar to her. Either way, I find myself craving these training sessions almost as much as I crave her body during our matings.

"These aren't calibrated for human hands," I tell her, making final adjustments to the circuit nodes that press against her fingertips. "But I've modified them to compensate for your smaller size and different neural pathways."

Quinn flexes her fingers, the gloves' metallic surface rippling like liquid mercury.

"They're lighter than they look," she says, turning her hands over to examine the pulsing conduits that run along her wrists.

My private tech lab has become our bonding space these past few days. A place where we explore something beyond the physical dominance that defines our encounters in the bedroom.

Here, I can share my knowledge, watch her mind work. It's fascinating. She who submits so beautifully beneath our bodies asserts herself here with questions that cut straight to the core of complex systems.

"Try activating the primary interface," I instruct, gesturing toward the neural-thread device sitting on the workbench. "Just like I showed you. Visualize the connection forming."

Quinn narrows her eyes in concentration, extending her gloved hand toward the device. For a moment, nothing happens. Then, a thin beam of blue light shoots from her palm, connecting with the neural interface.

The device hums to life, its display spinning out a complex web of data symbols.

"Holy shit, it worked!" She laughs, her face lighting up with pride.

That expression on her face sends a bright warmth through my chest.

"Your neural patterns are becoming more compatible with our tech," I observe, studying the readouts. "The gloves are adapting to you."

"More like I'm making them my bitch." Quinn's eyes meet mine, challenging me as always.

My skin patterns flicker in response.

I've laid out an array of mid-level Drayzok tech for today's session. They're all items that are complex enough to be useful, but not so advanced that Quinn can't grasp their function.

The stealth emitter sits beside the pulse blade, both dwarfed by the neural-thread access device that now pulses with Quinn's biorhythms.

"What's this one do?" She points to the stealth emitter, a hexagonal device no bigger than her palm.

"It creates a disruption field that bends light around the user," I explain, picking it up and placing it in her gloved hand. "Temporary invisibility, essentially. It's not perfect—movement creates distortion patterns—but effective for brief tactical advantages."

Quinn's eyes widen. "Actual invisibility? Geez, I feel like I'm in the science fiction section of my old library."

"Many of your 'fictions' are quite achievable with the right application of energy manipulation," I tell her, enjoying her fascination. It's one of the many things that draws me to her, this hunger for knowledge that mirrors my own.

I watch as she activates the stealth emitter, making her form shimmer for a moment before partially disappearing.

She's not completely invisible. It's more like a heat mirage, a distortion in the air that gives away her presence if you know what to look for. But it's an impressive first attempt.

"I can still see parts of myself," she says, examining her semi-transparent arm.

"The field needs to calibrate to your specific biological signature." I step closer. "Each use will improve its efficiency. Try moving."

She takes a few steps, and I track the rippling distortion in the air. When she deactivates the device, she reappears with a grin that makes my chest tighten oddly.

"That is seriously cool," she says, setting the emitter down with a gentleness that suggests respect for the technology. "What would happen if I tried to use it while running?"

"The field would collapse from the energy distortion. It's meant for stealth, not sustained evasion."

Quinn nods, absorbing this information thoughtfully.

Her thoughtfulness doesn't surprise me anymore. When we first brought her here, I believed the manuals, which indicated that she would be incapable of understanding our technology. That human females are intellectually inferior.

Yet another falsehood in those damned texts.

She's been spending time with each of us differently. Zegran told me she's been asking him about Draxith, about our customs and history back on the homeworld.

She shares stories of her own world in return. Tales of survival in Earth's harsh landscape, of trading outposts and human communities clinging to existence.

Korvan comes back from their combat sessions with bruises and a look of pride, boasting about Quinn's quick reflexes and creative fighting style.

With me, it's technology and science. She asks questions no human female is supposed to comprehend, let alone care about. Her fingers brush my wrist when I correct her grip on a device, and the casual touch sends my skin patterns surging in response.

"Let's try the pulse blade," I suggest, moving toward the weapon.

It's a simple design. A hilt containing a power core that generates a short-range energy blade. Not nearly as powerful as our standard combat weapons, but lethal enough in skilled hands.

Quinn picks it up, testing its weight. "This is lighter than it looks, too."

"Activate it by pressing your thumb against the recognition pad and visualizing an extension of your arm."

She follows my instructions, and the blade flares to life, a crackling line of blue energy extending about the length of her forearm. It hums with barely contained power, giving her face a glow that accentuates her stunning features.

The door to my lab hisses open without warning, and Korvan strides in. His eyes light up at the sight of Quinn wielding the pulse blade.

"Thought I heard that." He grins, moving toward us. "Finally teaching her something useful, eh?"

"We're in the middle of a training session." My irritation flares at the interruption.

Korvan ignores me, circling Quinn with appraising eyes.

"Let's see what you've learned, little human." He plucks the blade from her hands, then tosses it back to her to see if she can figure out how to reactivate it.

"I was explaining the proper technique for—" I begin, but Korvan cuts me off.

"Theory is worthless without practice." He turns to Quinn, his stance widening into a combat-ready position. "Show me what Thalor's been teaching you. Better yet, show me what you've learned in our combat drills."

Quinn laughs. She still surprises me sometimes with the lack of fear in her laugh.

"You sure you want that?" she asks Korvan. "I knocked you on your ass yesterday."

"You got lucky," Korvan growls, but there's no real anger in it. Just a playful challenge.

I should be annoyed at this disruption of my carefully planned lesson, but watching Quinn slip into a fighting stance—her body moving with newfound confidence—sends a different kind of heat through my circuits.

"Don't damage my equipment," I warn, moving my more delicate devices to a safer location.

"Worried about your toys?" Korvan taunts. "Or worried I'll show your student a thing or two you can't teach her?"

"Maybe you should both worry about me," Quinn interjects, her blade whirring as she spins it in a controlled arc.

That's all the warning we get before she lunges at Korvan, the pulse blade slicing through the air where his chest was a moment before. He dodges, laughing as he counters with a deliberately slow strike that she easily parries.

He's playing with her, I realize. Testing her reflexes without actually risking harm.

But Quinn isn't just playing. She's learning, adapting with each movement. She incorporates the technical knowledge I've given her about the blade's energy field with the combat techniques Korvan's been drilling into her.

I find myself drawn into their dance, picking up a training staff from the wall rack.

"Your form is sloppy," I tell Korvan, sliding between them with a strike that forces him back. "You're leaving your right flank exposed."

"Then come fix it," he challenges, and suddenly we're all engaged in a three-way sparring match that transforms my orderly lab into an impromptu combat arena.

Quinn is breathless, flushed, her pink skin slick with sweat that makes her whole body glisten. She dodges my staff, rolls under Korvan's blade, and comes up laughing.

There's joy in her movements now, none of the desperate terror that marked her early attempts to escape us.

I'm struck again by how different she looks from the helpless captive we first claimed. Her body moves with purpose, with confidence.

The curve of her hip as she pivots from Korvan's reach, the strength in her thighs as she launches herself over my low sweep—all of it speaks to a woman coming into her power.

"You're thinking too much, Thalor!" she taunts as she slips past my guard, the training blade stopping just short of my ribs. "All that brain and no instinct."

Korvan bellows with laughter at my expense, but I don't mind. I'm too fascinated by this side of Quinn. Playful, provocative, and pushing us as much as we push her.

The door slides open again, and this time it's Zegran who enters, his spines fully extended in curiosity.

He observes our chaotic skirmish with narrowed eyes and rigid posture.

"What is this?" he demands. He's pretending to keep his distance, but the flush of biolights creeping up his neck shows his interest.

"Combat training," Korvan answers, not pausing in his assault on Quinn's defenses.

"Technology lessons," I correct, deflecting Quinn's blade with a twist of my staff.

"Looks like neither to me," Zegran says, stepping into our circle. "It looks like you're both being outmaneuvered by our mate."

As if to prove his point, Quinn lands a solid hit on Korvan's shoulder, making him grunt in surprise. She spins away before he can retaliate, a triumphant grin on her face.

"Maybe you should join us, then," she challenges Zegran directly. "Or are you not strong enough to show 'em how it's done?"

I tense. Our leader does not tolerate mockery, even in friendly jest.

But to my shock, his mouth melts into a smile, light patterns pulsing with heightened interest.

"Perhaps I will," he says, drawing his own blade—a full-sized combat weapon that dwarfs Quinn's training model. "Perhaps it's time our mate learned what a true fighter feels like."

Quinn doesn't back down. If anything, her stance becomes more defiant, more provocative.

"Big talk from someone who hasn't landed a hit yet."

Zegran's spines quiver with excitement. When did this happen? When did our leader start enjoying Quinn's defiance rather than punishing it?

The combat resumes, now with Zegran at its center. His movements are controlled power, holding back his full strength but still pressing Quinn harder than Korvan or I dared.

She responds with increasing intensity, her body gleaming with exertion, her eyes bright with challenge.

None of us is surprised when our "combat" begins to look more like what Quinn calls "foreplay." The clash of wills, the testing of boundaries, the physical struggle for dominance—it's all part of the dance that leads to our matings.

Quinn seems to crave it as much as we do, this ritual of resistance and conquest.

Zegran catches Quinn's elbow, disarming her with a twist that brings her body flush against his.

She doesn't yield, driving her elbow back toward his ribs, but Korvan is right beside her, capturing her other arm and pinning it behind her back.

I move to complete the circle, stepping in to trap her legs with mine. She's immobilized between the three of us, her chest heaving, her eyes dark with the same desire that courses through my veins.

"Yield," Zegran commands, his voice rough.

"Make me."

It's the same game we've played nearly every night since giving her the translator chip. The same defiance that ignites our primal need to claim and possess.

What follows is familiar, too. The struggle that isn't really a struggle, the conquest that Quinn eventually admits she's craved all along.

We overpower her, just as she wants us to. She fights back, just as we need her to. Our clothes are discarded, scattered across my lab floor as we claim her, each in our own way.

Zegran takes her first, which is his right as the one who joined the fight and took control from her.

I watch her face as he enters her, her resistance melting into pleasure that flushes her cheeks pink.

When he finishes, Korvan follows, and then me. Through it all, Quinn meets us with a fire that no amount of claiming seems to extinguish.

After we've all finished and Quinn is thoroughly soaked in our seed, we all collapse down on the padded mat I keep for extended work sessions.

Quinn is curled between Korvan and me. Her body is soft and spent, her breathing slowing as she drifts toward sleep. Zegran lies beside us, one hand stroking her hair.

It feels right, having her here with us. Like pieces fitting together that I didn't know were meant to connect. In these moments, with her sleeping so contentedly among us, I can almost forget the complications that lie ahead.

Tomorrow is the public punishment of the warriors who tried to claim Quinn during her escape.

Drayzok justice is not gentle. It's not merciful. It's designed to make examples, to reinforce hierarchies through blood and pain.

Quinn knows it's happening—we've explained the process—but knowing and seeing are different things. I watch the peaceful rise and fall of her chest and wonder how she'll look at us tomorrow, after she witnesses what we're capable of. After she sees the violence we've been trained to inflict.

Will she still smile at me when I correct her grip on a tech device? Will she still laugh when Korvan teases her during combat drills? Will she still look at Zegran with that defiant spark that somehow earned his respect instead of his wrath?

Or will she remember that we are not human, that our ways are not her ways? Will she see us as monstrous once again?

I stroke the soft curve of her hip, memorizing the feel of her warm skin against mine.

I just hope our connection is strong enough to survive what comes next.

CHAPTER 20

KORVAN

I roll my shoulders back, feeling the weight of the ceremonial blade at my hip. The tribunal ground stretches before us, cold stone and ancient tradition. The ground is packed with warriors from our unit, all of them standing at attention with spines rigid and eyes forward.

But my gaze keeps drifting to Quinn.

Drayzok justice isn't pretty, but it's necessary. Is she prepared for what she's about to witness?

Quinn stands off to the side. She clutches the edge of her tunic, a simple garment that hangs loosely on her curved frame. The fabric is Drayzok-made, designed for our females, and it drapes differently over her fuller figure.

She doesn't belong here, but she insisted on coming. Said she needed to understand our ways. Now, I'm not so sure this was the right call.

I step to the center of the platform, handing Zegran the ceremonial blade. He takes it with his spines fully extended. A display of dominance that comes naturally to our Iron Guardian leader.

Thalor's stance is more measured, his eyes scanning the gathered warriors with that analytical sharpness that misses nothing.

Quinn darts her eyes around, taking in everything—the raised platform, the warriors standing in formation, the ceremonial weapons laid out. I wonder if she regrets insisting on attending, despite our warnings.

"It's my right to know," she'd said, lifting her chin. "If I'm supposed to be part of your world, I need to see all of it. Not just the parts you think I can handle."

I couldn't argue with that logic. None of us could.

The warriors of our unit stand before us in tight rows. Some remain still, eyes forward, but others shift uneasily, patterns flickering with suppressed emotion.

They know what's coming. They've seen punishment rituals before. Some have even experienced them firsthand.

But this one is different. This one is for Quinn.

But I still think she should be back in our quarters, safe and sated. She shouldn't be here, amidst this ritual of blood and pain. The thought makes me crack my neck, tension building in my muscles.

It's been several days since we gave her the translator chip. And by the stars, it's changed everything. She asks questions. She challenges us. She makes us explain ourselves.

And somehow, instead of punishing her defiance, we find ourselves wanting to answer. Wanting her to understand.

"Don't look at her," Zegran murmurs, too low for anyone but Thalor and me to hear. "Focus on the task at hand."

I grunt in acknowledgment, but my eyes find her one more time. She looks small among us, but at least I know she's not weak.

There's nothing about our mate that is weak.

Five warriors are marched forward, their hands bound before them. Their heads are low. I recognize two of them immediately—the ones who almost had their hands on Quinn when we saw them in the dining hall. Their patterns glowed with lust as they reached for her trembling, naked body.

The memory makes a growl rise in my throat.

These were the five from our unit who participated that day. So it's our job to punish them.

And everyone knows they'll be receiving the harshest punishment of all.

"Begin," Zegran commands, and a hush falls over the assembly.

Thalor steps forward, data pad in hand.

"We gather today to address a grave violation of our code," he announces, his voice carrying across the tribunal ground. "These five warriors stand accused of direct violation of claiming rights. You attempted to seize and claim a human female already assigned to superior officers. You continued your attempts even after direct orders to stand down."

I tighten my fists at my sides. I would've killed them all that day if Zegran hadn't focused us on getting Quinn out first.

"The human female Quinn Morgyn belongs to our trio. To Zegran Volkos, to myself Thalor Vorrek, and to Korvan Drek. She is under our protection. She is our mate."

I can feel Quinn stir slightly from the side. I don't know how she's feeling, but my chest is swelling at the public declaration that she is ours.

"By attempting to claim what is not yours, you have violated our most sacred laws," Thalor concludes. "The punishment will be administered according to rank and severity of offense."

Quinn shifts her weight from one foot to the other. I catch her gaze for just a moment, and she blinks quickly before looking back at the grounds.

Zegran descends the steps with measured strides, his authority unchallenged as he approaches the first warrior. The ceremonial blade gleams in his hand, its edge honed to perfect sharpness.

The warrior's chest is already bare, as tradition dictates. Zegran doesn't hesitate. In a movement almost too quick to follow, Zegran slashes across the warrior's chest.

Blood beads instantly, dark against blue flesh. The warrior grunts, but doesn't flinch. It's a point of pride not to show weakness during punishment.

But it's the sound from Quinn that gets my attention. I hear her gasp clearly, though she tries to stifle it behind her hand. When I look over, her face has gone pale, eyes wide.

Fuck. Frax. She wasn't ready for this, no matter what she claimed. Humans don't understand the necessity of blood justice.

Zegran completes his ritual strikes. Five in total. When he steps back, the warrior's chest is crossed with bleeding lines, his skin patterns pulsing weakly around the wounds.

Zegran turns and motions to me. My turn.

I take the blade without hesitation, feeling its perfect balance in my hand. The second warrior watches me approach, his eyes narrowing. I know this one well—he's been trouble since he joined our unit, questioning orders, pushing boundaries.

And he's one of the ones I recognized in the dining hall that day, his hands just inches away from gripping our mate.

"You were the first to reach for her," I say in a low growl. "You nearly touched her."

"She smelled ripe," he replies, smirking. "Sweet. Ready."

I don't hold back. The first blow lands with all my strength behind it, the crack echoing across the tribunal ground as it splits skin and glances off the hard muscle beneath. Blood sprays in a fine mist, spattering my chest and face. It's cold and smells of metal and rage.

The warrior staggers slightly but rights himself, eyes locked forward, jaw clenched against the pain.

Unlike Zegran's measured discipline, mine is raw power.

My second strike crosses the first, forming an 'X' that marks him as a failed challenger. More blood flows, running in rivulets down his torso to stain the waistband of his uniform pants.

As I pull back for the third strike, I glance toward Quinn again. She has her arms crossed tight across her chest, fists clenched so hard I can see her knuckles whitening from here. She's not looking away—I'll give her credit for that—but her breathing is shallow, her skin ashen.

I hesitate. This is our way. This is justice. This is how we maintain order in a society of warriors.

But through her eyes, I'm suddenly seeing it differently. I'm seeing the brutality, the blood, the violence of it all.

Something twists in my gut. Not regret for the punishment—these bastards deserve every cut and more for daring to touch what's mine. But regret that she has to see this side of us. The violent, brutal side.

The blade feels suddenly heavy in my hand.

I deliver the third strike with slightly less force than the previous two. The warrior still rocks back on his heels, a hiss escaping through clenched teeth.

As I raise my arm for the fourth and final blow, I pause, just for a heartbeat.

Then I remember how she looked in that dining hall. Scared. Trembling. Vulnerable.

These animals would have torn her apart in their frenzy.

My rage returns, washing away doubt, and I deliver the final strike with enough force to make the warrior finally stagger to his knees.

"Get up," I snarl. "Take your punishment like a warrior."

He rises slowly, blood streaming down his torso, his patterns dim with pain and shame. I step back, satisfied, and pass the blade to Thalor.

Thalor addresses the third warrior with a clinical detachment, explaining exactly why each strike is necessary and what it symbolizes. Then he delivers his blows. Clean, efficient, without flourish or fury. The warrior barely reacts, knowing that stoicism is his only dignity now.

Before the last two warriors, Zegran gives me a nod. Together, we take position on either side of the fourth warrior, the blade passing between us as we deliver alternating strikes. Left, right, left, right, a choreography of punishment that leaves the warrior trembling, but upright.

Then comes the last one. The ringleader, a veteran who should have known better.

His punishment falls to Zegran. Leader taking on leader.

The warrior raises his chin, meeting Zegran's gaze as he approaches. My patterns pulse with anger.

"You led them," Zegran states.

"I did what any unmated warrior would do," the accused replies, his voice carrying across the suddenly silent ground. "The human was unclaimed. Undefended."

A murmur ripples through the assembly. I hear Quinn's sharp intake of breath.

"She was claimed," Zegran says. His voice is dangerously soft. "She was ours from the moment we brought her aboard. Your actions dishonored not only our trio, but all Drayzok warriors."

He lifts the ceremonial blade.

For this warrior, it's not just a strike. Not a momentary blow for him to wince at and immediately begin healing from.

When Zegran brings his blade to the warrior's chest, he keeps it there, pressing into the wound he's created and watching the blood rise.

"Argh!" The warrior can't help squealing like swine. It's satisfying to hear.

Zegran steps back and nods at Thalor and me. He wants us each to have a part in this one's punishment.

I push forward, grabbing the blade before Thalor and slashing it across the warrior's skin. Blood sprays, splattering the stone at our feet.

Thalor follows with a strike that crosses mine. Back and forth we go, passing the blade between us.

By the sixth strike, the warrior is on his knees, blood pooling beneath him on the stone. He's breathing in ragged gasps.

Zegran finishes with a final strike, one that will truly shame the warrior. It lands across his back. The scar will mark him forever, showing that he turned away from his punishment rather than facing it like a true fighter.

The scent of blood fills the air, sharp and honest. It's a clean smell, the smell of justice served.

Quinn makes a small sound, barely audible over the breathing of the assembled warriors. But to me, it's like a scream cutting through the ritual.

She's not made for this. Not hardened to it like we are.

Zegran returns to the center of the platform, blood spattered across his chest and arms, the ceremonial blade dripping dark red in his hand.

He addresses the crowd with a brief command: "Let this be remembered. She is ours. Her safety is law."

Thalor closes the ritual with a formal invocation that returns justice to our unit. His words are ancient, handed down through generations of Drayzok warriors, binding us all to the verdict delivered here today.

The crowd disperses, warriors filing out in formation. The punished are removed for healing. Their wounds will be treated, but the scars will remain, a permanent reminder of their transgression.

Some may never regain their former status. Others might work twice as hard to prove themselves worthy again.

That's their choice now.

Quinn doesn't move. She stands frozen, her eyes open but unfocused, as if she's seeing something far away.

When the tribunal ground is nearly empty, I approach her with an outstretched hand. Blood stains my skin, drying in black smears across my knuckles.

She jerks away from me. The rejection stings more than I'd like to admit.

"I didn't know it would be like this," she says quietly. Her voice is broken, and that cracks something open in my chest.

Zegran approaches, his face and chest still smeared with the warriors' blood. He sees Quinn's distress and stops, uncertain for the first time since I've known him. Our leader, always so sure, now stands hesitant before this small human female.

Thalor moves forward, ready to explain. "Quinn, you must understand the cultural context—"

I raise my hand, stopping him. This isn't about logic or reason. This is about something more primal.

"This is how we keep order," I tell her. "Those warriors? They would have done worse to you."

She looks between the three of us, distrust on her face.

"Is this what happens to anyone who breaks your rules?" she asks, her voice steadier now.

"Our way ensures that everyone knows their place," I say. "That boundaries are respected. Those warriors will never approach you again. No warrior who witnessed today will ever think of claiming you."

"Because I'm your property," she says. There's bitterness in her voice.

It's not really a question, but I answer anyway. "You're ours."

She looks at all three of us like she's seeing something she hadn't wanted to. Like we've disappointed her in some fundamental way.

The distance between us, which had been shrinking in recent days, suddenly stretches wide again.

"I need some time," she says finally, then turns and walks away, quickly disappearing into the corridor leading back to our quarters.

I watch her go, bringing my hand to my chest. I don't regret the punishment. Those warriors deserved their marks.

But I regret that it's cost us something with Quinn.

Which means we could lose her, simply because of who we are.

CHAPTER 21

QUINN

I press my forehead against the ice-cold glass of the observation deck window, watching stars streak past like tears.

My stomach's still turning from what I just saw: blades flashing, blue skin splitting open, blood so dark, it was almost black, splattering against stone.

The sharp smell of it is still hanging out in my nostrils, and I might start huffing walls around here just to smell something else.

It was my guys who did that. My captors. Or mates? Whatever the hell they are to me now.

They did that, and they did it for me. Because of me.

And of course, I'm the genius who had to go insisting that they do it right in front of me.

God, the sounds. The crack of the blade hitting flesh. The way the warriors grunted, trying to keep a straight face while they got punished.

The audience just stood there, some of them even murmuring in approval, like this was a damn picnic at the drive-in.

I squeeze my eyes shut, but that just cranks the images up to eleven.

Korvan's face is what haunts me most. That flat, emotionless expression as he carved into another living body. Thalor did it like that too, like he was chopping vegetables, not slicing open someone's chest.

Zegran, at least, showed some fury, but now that I think about it, I'm not sure which way is worse.

Look, I'm no stranger to violence. I lived through the collapse of civilization on Earth, when you had to bash heads for food or anything else you wanted to keep.

I've done it myself, pulling out the violence. I'm no angel here. Hell, the last thing I did on Earth included delivering a paintball to an eyeball.

But this? This Drayzok thing? This was different.

It wasn't about survival. It wasn't even a fight. This was... ceremony. Violence with a script and an audience.

They made a whole pageant out of being brutal. What kind of society functions like that?

A shiver runs through me as I remember the way those five warriors looked at me during the ceremony. No remorse in their eyes. Just anger at being caught, at belonging to the wrong trio, at not being strong enough to take what they wanted.

I shove off the window and start pacing the deck. Thank god nobody's here. It's just me and the endless black, with my own reflection watching me from the window. That reflection shows a clean stranger in alien clothes, someone who's been getting fucked by the very monsters I once cursed.

And liking it.

I press my palms into my eyes until I see stars. At first, it was simple. They were the monsters, I was their captive.

Then came the translation chip. Suddenly they had names. Zegran, with his take-charge attitude and that hidden softness. Thalor, always poking at gadgets, always trying to figure stuff out. Korvan, all muscle and protectiveness and, hell, sometimes even a sense of humor.

I got used to them. Started to feel safe. Even craved the sex. Maybe I even liked... them. It wasn't just about their glowing dicks. I actually started to fall for them.

Started to feel like maybe this new life wasn't so bad after all.

What a fucking joke.

How do I know my guys are really any different from the Rust Rats? Right now, they sure seem like people who enjoy violence just for the joy of cruelty.

These are the guys I let inside me. The ones I was starting to trust.

I've been selfish. Focused on my own survival, my own comfort. So much that I missed what's really going on.

I shudder, wrapping my arms around myself. Am I really safe with them? Or am I just a pet they're guarding? A fancy toy they don't want anyone else to break?

My thoughts shoot back to Katarina, to the rage that hit me at the trading post when Estelle told me the Rust Rats had sold Katarina to the Drayzok. Me and Kat had a few things in common, like being big girls.

But Katarina's better than me, in that she's actually a nice person. Still sweet, somehow, even in this universe with all its fucked up monsters, human and alien both.

Where is she now? Is she strapped to a table somewhere on this station, getting the "fral'ra" treatment? Is she screaming for help in a language no one cares to understand?

I almost gag. Because that could've been me. Would've been me, if not for...

The chip.

I touch the barely-there bump on the back of my neck where they injected the translator device. Such a small thing, but it changed everything. It gave me a voice.

And my monsters listened. They actually listened.

Other women, like Katarina, they don't get that chance.

The guilt hits so hard I have to sit. Here I am, living it up. Nice quarters. Training. All the food I want. Clothes.

I'm even enjoying the sex, rough and dominating as my guys are.

Meanwhile, the rest of them are still stuck in a nightmare.

The difference is this tiny translator chip. That's the key.

Every woman needs one. A way to speak, to be heard.

I get up, knowing what I'm gonna do. I have to tell them. My trio broke the rules for me, so maybe they'll help me do it again.

I practically sprint through the corridors back to our shared quarters, my mind racing ahead of my feet. They'll understand, won't they? They've changed since I got the chip. They've listened to me. They believe in my ideas.

Rushing into our quarters, I find them all in the main living area, clustered around a floating hologram that's spitting out data points. They look up when I enter, and something in my expression must give me away, because Thalor instantly sets aside his data pad.

"Quinn," he says. "We were beginning to worry."

"I'm fine," I say, waving away his concern. "Listen, I need to talk to you. It's important."

Zegran's spines snap up in that way I now know means he's paying attention. "Speak, then."

I suck in a breath, organizing my thoughts. "The translator chip changed everything for me," I begin. "Before it, I was... well, scared shitless. Confused. I didn't understand what you wanted or why you were doing those things to me."

Korvan shifts uncomfortably, his circular patterns dimming slightly. Good. At least they've got the decency to feel shame.

"But after the chip, we could actually communicate," I continue. "I could tell you what I wanted, what scared me. You could explain your customs. It wasn't perfect, but it was... better."

Thalor nods, encouraging me to go on.

"So I've been thinking," I say, my voice growing stronger. "What if all the human women had chips? What if they could talk to their captors—I mean, their mates—the way I can talk to you?"

Instant reaction. Zegran's spines go stiff.

"That is not possible," he says, flat.

"Why not?" I push. "You did it for me. It changed everything between us."

"Quinn." Thalor's eyes are dark. "The translator chip we acquired for you was against regulations. It required... significant risk and violation of protocols."

"We broke the law," Korvan adds bluntly, crossing his arms. "It's not just frowned upon. It's expressly forbidden to give human females this technology."

"But you know the rules are bullshit," I remind them.

"The laws are clear," Zegran states firmly. "The Council has decreed it. This technology is strictly controlled by the Technician Order."

"So you just follow orders? Even when you know they're wrong?" I'm practically yelling.

"It's not that simple," Thalor says, looking miserable. "These laws are foundational to our society's structure. Breaking them once, for you—that was a risk we willingly took. What you're asking for, it's not just breaking the rules. It's tearing them down."

"It's impossible." Zegran's tone is final. "Getting your chip was a one-time deal. I won't—can't—do it again. Not on the scale you're suggesting."

I look to Korvan, hoping for support. He just shakes his head.

"There are thousands of human females across our territories," he says quietly. "The resources it would take are entirely too much."

That's it, then. They won't help. It's over.

No matter how far we've come, no matter how much they claim to care for me, I'm still just a thing to them. Just their possession they'd do anything to keep, but as far as who I am? What being human means?

It doesn't matter to them.

"I get it." My voice is weirdly calm. "Thank you for clarifying where I stand."

"Quinn," Thalor says, reaching for me. I step back.

"I'm tired," I tell them. "I think I need some rest."

They look at each other. Maybe they get how I'm feeling. Maybe they don't really care.

In the personal room they've given me, with the door shut, I let myself have one shuddering breath. One moment to feel it.

Then, I start planning.

I look around the small room. They've given me a few luxuries. Soft bedding, some decorative items, a data pad for entertainment.

Little comforts to keep their pet content.

But they've also grown complacent, confident in their ownership of me. They trust me now.

Their mistake.

I move to the small storage unit where I've been collecting bits and pieces of tech over the past weeks. Nothing obvious, just components I've claimed interest in for "human curiosity."

I know their tech now. Just enough of it, anyway, thanks to Thalor's lessons. And thanks to the translation chip, I can read their language, enough to operate their basic systems. I know how to find the transport pods.

And I know exactly what I have to do.

I stuff a data pad in my tunic. Grab the stealth emitter. Program a locator with Earth coordinates.

Specifically, the area where Estelle's trading post should be. If she's still operating there, she'll be my best chance at spreading the word. She might be a hard-ass, but she cares about other women in her own gruff way. She'll understand what needs to be done.

I almost leave a note for my captors on the comm pad.

"I didn't want to leave like this. But I had to. You'll understand one day."

No, that's not right. I delete it, try again.

"This isn't about me. It's about all those women."

That's not right either. Delete.

Screw it. Nothing I say will fix this.

It's too easy for me to slip out of the living quarters. My trio's not guarding me anymore. Why would they? I've been transforming into the perfect compliant mate.

Until now.

In the corridor, I flick the stealth emitter on. My body shimmers, not quite invisible, but enough to fool anyone who isn't looking close.

Gotta move slow. Thalor warned me.

Step by step, I make my way to the transport bay.

Each step forward is one more step away from them. From Zegran, who surprised me with kindness. From Thalor, always curious. From Korvan, who held me at night.

But each step also takes me closer to Earth. To Estelle. To spreading the word that could save countless women from unnecessary suffering.

At the port gate, a drone scans the hallway. I wait, holding my breath. It moves on.

I slide through a maintenance panel, using the code I stole.

There's a small vessel, a transport pod. Not for long trips, but enough to get to the surface. I've studied the simple controls during Thalor's lessons.

I can do this.

Just as I step on board, for one long second, I almost turn back. I think about their arms, their warmth, the weird comfort I've found in them.

Then I think of Katarina. Of everyone like her.

"I'm sorry," I whisper, though there's no one to hear me. "But this is bigger than us."

I launch myself into darkness, leaving my trio behind.

CHAPTER 22

QUINN

Dust hangs in the air of Estelle's trading post, just like it did before I was taken. She moved her spot after I left, but she didn't go far, and so much of it is exactly the same.

The worn-down merchandise. The rusty metal smell. The weird incense she burns to "keep out the bad vibes."

It's like I never left.

But I sure can't forget that I did. It's not easy to forget I've spent weeks getting fucked by aliens.

And it's not easy getting stared down by Estelle's suspicious face right now.

Her voice is as rough as the gravel outside. "So you're telling me these translation... doohickies—"

"Chips."

"Chips." She coughs. "You're telling me these translation chips are the answer? Give every woman one and the Drayzok will stop treating 'em like animals?"

She wraps her gnarled fingers around a chipped mug of something that smells suspiciously like engine coolant but is probably just her homemade hooch.

I lean in, trying to get across how urgent this is. "It changed every-thing, Estelle. Once they could actually understand me—once I could tell them the way they were treating me wasn't okay—they listened."

"Listened," she repeats flatly. Her eyes go sharp in a web of wrinkles. "And what exactly were they doing that wasn't 'okay'?"

My face goes hot. No way am I giving Estelle the details about the fral'ra process, or how my body totally got on board with it. Some things are better left unsaid.

"Look, point is, there's been a huge misunderstanding. The Dray-zok, they were told by the Original Agents that human women are..." I fumble for the right words. "That we're into being conquered with sex, basically. The Original Agents said we'd resist them only because that's some sex game we like to play."

Estelle snorts. "And you believed that pile of shit? That they just didn't know any better?" She rocks her chair back, and the thing creaks ominously. "Girl, I remember how you used to talk about those blue bastards. I used to think you might be the only one who hated those fuckers more than me."

I swallow hard. Yeah, that was me, all right.

"I remember," I say, quieter now.

"So what changed?" Estelle's eyes pin me. "Because you know what I thought when I heard they took you? I said to myself, 'Shit, Quinn's up there giving 'em hell.' I figured, if anybody, you'd be the one to find a way out."

She spits. "And look. I was right. Except instead of trying to take those motherfuckers down, you're trying to get us all to... What? Sit down and talk to 'em over tea?"

She repeats the question: "What changed, Quinn?"

What changed? Me. Them. Everything.

"It's complicated."

"Un-complicate it."

I try to gulp, but my mouth has gone dry, and the truth is stuck in my throat. How do I tell Estelle what all my big talk was really about?

All my vicious hate for the Drayzok was partly just a cover. Partly just hate for myself. Because I'd felt like there was something wrong and twisted about the way I fantasized about them. About being at the mercy of someone so powerful.

And then it happened. And it was awful. And then it was... not.

"Look," I say, "all that matters is, I found out something important. The Drayzok, they're not all evil. Some of them are misguided. The Original Agents lied to them, and they honestly think they're doing what human women want. Without the translation chips, they'll never find out what we really want."

"And what do 'we' want, Quinn? Because last I checked, we wanted those fuckwipes to leave us the hell alone."

My trio's faces flash through my mind. The last thing I'd want? Them leaving me the hell alone.

But that might be exactly what they're gonna do now. I left them, and I don't even know if they'll want me back after I did.

I'll probably never again see Zegran's spines quiver when I challenge him. Or feel Thalor's careful fingers adjusting tech for my size. Or sleep with Korvan curled around me like a big, grumpy teddy bear.

There's a lump in my throat.

I swallow it down to reply. "Yeah, some women do want the Drayzok to leave them alone, of course. But others might choose differently if they got the chance to actually talk. If they could make the Drayzok understand we're not what the Original Agents said."

Estelle studies me for a long moment.

"So these translation chips," she says finally. "You brought some with you to hand out?"

And there's the flaw in my genius plan. I wince. "No. They're restricted technology. The one I have was stolen, and it almost got my..." I stop myself. "It almost got those Drayzok in trouble."

Estelle's eyebrows shoot up. "So your big plan is to tell women to get chips that are impossible to get?"

"Not impossible," I argue, but it's weak. "Difficult, yeah. But if a woman can figure out how to find one, or- I don't know, demand one..."

She barks out a laugh. "And you think they'll just hand it over to a shy girl like Katarina because she asks nicely? You've got guts, girl, I'll give you that. Always did. But this plan of yours has more holes than my roof after that hailstorm last spring."

Frustration makes my face burn. "What's your better idea, then? Just let things keep going as they are? Let women be taken without zero chance of being understood?"

"No." Estelle softens her voice, but not by much. "But you gotta give people more than just information. You gotta give them a way to use it."

She's right, and I know it. I rub my temples. My head's starting to ache.

"I didn't think it through," I admit. "I just wanted to do something, anything... Just wanted to help."

Estelle nods. It's the closest I've ever seen to her looking at me with sympathy.

"You always were a soft touch under all that bluster," she says. "I'll do what I can to spread the word about the chips. Not that I have many female customers left these days. The Rust Rats have scared most of them into hiding."

I let out a breath. It's not much, but it's a start. "Thank you."

"And, hey. It's a big first step you took. You got out, you did this much. That's something to be proud of."

I can't just shrug that off, as much as I could try. Because a genuine compliment from Estelle is as rare as a generous trade from her.

That lump is back in my throat.

Shit. My emotions are all over the place. I need a distraction.

I grab the container I packed back on the Drayzok station and slide it across the table.

"What's this?" Estelle peers inside.

"Drayzok tech that I, uh, borrowed before I left. Might be useful."

She eyes the container like it's full of snakes, so I pick up a few items to show they don't bite.

"This one," I say, lifting a small disc, "can disrupt security systems for about thirty seconds. And this..." I pick up what looks like a smooth black pebble. "This can heal minor wounds."

Estelle lifts her eyes to my face. "How'd you get all this?"

I think of Thalor's patient explanations, his pride as he showed me his designs. The way his patterns would glow brighter when I asked questions.

My chest tightens.

"I had a good tech teacher," is all I say.

"And what about me? What am I supposed to do with alien gadgets I don't understand?"

"I don't know, Estelle, I thought you could figure it out. Trade them. Keep them safe until someone needs them. I'm making this up as I go, okay?"

"Fair enough." She nods slowly, closing the container with careful hands. "This 'teacher' of yours. Is that who made you wanna talk to the Drayzok instead of kicking their blue asses?"

I sigh. "They're not all monsters."

She grunts skeptically. "And what exactly did they put you through up there? These not-monsters of yours?"

Things that would give a normal person nightmares, I want to say. Ten minutes back on Earth, and I'm already ashamed of my fantasies again.

What did my captors do to me? Restrained me. Stripped me down, in more ways than one. Before they gave me a voice. Listened. Protected me.

And still dominated me, yes. But even in that, they cared for me. And I cared for them.

And then I left them.

They'll never forgive that betrayal. They'll never want me back, not after I spat in the face of everything they believe about hierarchy and loyalty and possession.

Could I even handle going back to them? It might not exactly be a happy reunion. By Drayzok rules, I should be in for serious punishment.

"Quinn?" Estelle prods.

"Like I said, it's complicated." I can't meet her eyes. Estelle would never get it.

Hell, I hardly get it myself. How do you miss your captors? How did that happen?

Estelle must see something in my face, because instead of pressing the question, she shifts in her chair and bends down behind the counter. When she straightens, she's holding a bundle wrapped in stained cloth.

"After you disappeared, the Rats were sprawled out like trash in the dirt. Once the Drayzok cleared out, I went picking through the mess. Figured someone oughta salvage what you left behind."

She unwraps the bundle, and my chest squeezes. It's the boots she gave me that day. Scuffed but solid. And Suzie—my ridiculous little paintball slingshot that helped me fight the Rust Rats.

"Your scooter, I sold," Estelle admits, defensive. "Worth too much to just let it sit around. But these? Couldn't bring myself to toss 'em. Maybe I thought you'd stomp back in here one day."

I touch Suzie's grip and trace the cracked leather of the boots. At one point, I treasured Suzie and coveted those boots like nothing else. But I feel disconnected from these items now. Like they're relics from a different life.

"Not mine anymore," I say, sliding them back across the counter. "Keep them. For the next girl who needs to fight back."

Estelle grunts, but she doesn't get a chance to press me to take them. Because we both hear a familiar sound just then.

Snarling male voices and tinkling chains. My blood chills.

"Rust Rats," Estelle hisses, going for the shotgun under her counter. "Back door. Now."

I'm moving in an instant, hand on the pulse blade under my jacket. "How many?"

"Too many," she grunts, checking the gun. "Probably spotted your transport pod. They've been wanting to get their hands on you since you disappeared. Calling for payback for that paintball stunt you pulled."

Great. Just perfect. I slide toward the back, keeping low. "You coming?"

Estelle gives me a look. "This is my shop. I don't run from rats."

I want to argue, but there's no time. The voices are close now, eager and angry. I slip out the back into the junkyard, a maze of rusted cars and scrap metal.

Crouching behind a burned-out truck, I watch eight Rust Rats spread through the yard. They're in their usual gear, worn leather with homemade blades attached.

Their leader is easy to spot. It's the same guy who tried to get me before. Now he's wearing an eyepatch.

I have to smile. Suzie must've done more damage than I thought.

She's with Estelle back in the shop, but I think she wouldn't mind stepping aside for my upgrade.

I grip the pulse blade and slide my thumb over the activation switch, just like Thalor taught me. The weapon vibrates to life, ready to act as an extension of my arm.

The Rust Rats haven't seen me yet, but they will.

Two of them move closer to my position, scanning the area with their crude headlamps. I steady my breaths, tapping into the combat breathing drills Korvan had me practice on repeat.

Wait for the moment. Let them come to you.

The first one's close enough to touch. I spring up. He doesn't even have time to shout before the pulse blade flashes, dropping him to the ground with barely a twitch.

The second guy whirls, eyes wide.

"It's her!" he screams. "She's over—"

He never finishes. I duck, roll behind him, and drop him too.

Korvan would approve.

"Over there!" someone else shouts, making the junkyard explode into motion.

I dart between scrap heaps, using the terrain for cover. Metal screeches as some dumbass Rust Rat tries to throw a blade at my head and misses, sending it ricocheting off an engine block instead.

I pop up behind a tire stack and fire. Another Rat down. I move before his body even hits the ground.

Two of them try to flank me from both sides. I sweep my arm through the air and hit them both with the pulse blade, one a second after the other.

First guy's stunned enough to wait for his pal before he falls, so they both go down in unison.

Oh, I really wish Korvan could see me right now. Thalor and Zegran, too. They'd all be proud.

Four down. Four left.

The leader's voice rises from somewhere among the scrap.

"Alien's whore!" he roars. "We'll take what's left of you to the highest bidder!"

He follows the trail of bodies until he spots me. I brace as he charges, ordering two of his men to follow.

The pulse blade is almost weightless in my hand. It feels deadly, but it also feels like an extension of my own body.

Like I'm the deadly one.

I fire into the leader's chest as he reaches me. He slumps down, and I make his body my shield as his two men try to stab me.

Then I slice right through him. The pulse blade cuts his body in two at the torso, spilling his guts onto his men just before they're cut down with him.

The last guy is smarter than his friends. He turns to run.

I almost let him. But I can't leave witnesses who might come back for Estelle.

A quick shot and he falls.

Silence settles over the junkyard. I'm breathing hard, the pulse blade still humming in my hand.

Eight men dead in just a couple of minutes. I should feel rattled, right?

I don't. Have I hardened that much during my time with the Dray-zok?

As I catch my breath, I switch off the pulse blade. But I still feel vibrating.

It's in the air.

I look up. A Drayzok shuttle drops from the clouds, spraying dust everywhere as it lands in the open field beyond the junkyard.

My heart pounds, fear and relief all crashing together. I already know it's not just any Drayzok on that shuttle.

The doors slide open. Three huge silhouettes fill the frame, lit from behind. Their light patterns pulse, weapons ready.

Zegran, Thalor, and Korvan scan the scene, quickly spotting me among the bodies.

I step forward, still clutching the pulse blade.

Zegran may be holding a weapon, but his face looks completely disarmed. His expression melts from fury to relief the closer he comes to me.

"Quinn. You're unharmed."

Thalor looks around at the dead Rust Rats and then back at me, glowing with approval. Korvan doesn't care about the dead, plowing over them as he takes the straightest route to me.

I lift my chin. "I had to warn them. Tell women about the translation chips, about what your people believe about us."

And what am I supposed to do now? Run from my captors?

Or stop calling them my "captors" and make a choice to go with them?

Korvan reaches for me, and in his arms, there's no other choice. His scent fills me, and I realize how much I missed it. Missed them.

I step into his grip, and he pulls me against his chest.

His light patterns are shimmering with tension. All of them are. I can feel how angry they are, even before I hear Zegran's growl.

"You will face consequences for your escape, little mate."

I shiver, but I don't look away. Whatever comes next, I'll face it.

CHAPTER 23

QUINN

The shuttle's restraints dig into my wrists, metal biting down with every damn jolt as we punch through Earth's atmosphere. Fresh pain shoots through my body, letting me feel all my souvenirs from my run-in with the Rust Rats.

But the ache in my muscles is nothing compared to the knot in my chest. My heart's a twisted-up mess of winning and losing at the same time.

I got the word to Estelle. Mission accomplished. So why does watching my three Drayzok approach make me feel like I've lost something I can't replace?

I wince, but I don't know if it makes a difference to these guys that the restraints are hurting me. Maybe that's the point. Maybe the pain's a little preview of what's to come.

Zegran, Thalor, and Korvan haven't said a word to me since we lifted off. Their silence is heavy.

They don't have to say anything for me to know they're angry. Zegran's spines are flared with stiff anger. I've never seen Korvan so still, like his muscles are waiting to leap into action. Thalor's light patterns flash in pissed-off streaks.

"Did you think we wouldn't find you?" Zegran's voice is low and dangerous. He holds his face inches from mine.

I tilt my chin. "Honestly? I thought you wouldn't bother."

Wrong answer. Zegran grabs my jaw hard, crushing my cheeks and forcing me to look up at him.

"Why would you say that? You don't know how we care for you?"

There's a crack in his voice that throws me off. He's not just angry. He's actually hurt.

"Why did you run?" Korvan demands to know. "After everything we shared with you. After we claimed you. Why?"

"I had to warn them." My voice comes out thick, muffled by Zegran's fingers. "Earth women need to know about the chips. They deserve a chance."

Thalor edges closer. "You could have told us. We would have listened."

"Would you?" I shoot back. "When I suggested getting chips for other women, you all shut me down. Said it was impossible."

"Because it is impossible!" Korvan's growl rattles the metal around me. "You have no idea what you're suggesting. The risk would be—"

"Too big for you," I snap, "but what about them? What about all the women being taken and violated because they can't even understand what's happening to them?"

Zegran's grip tightens. "And what of us? Did we mean nothing to you?"

That one stings. I was ready for yelling. Ready for consequences.

Not ready for them to sound hurt.

"I..." I falter. How the hell do I say that leaving them was like tearing off a piece of myself? That every second I was away from them felt wrong? "It wasn't about you. It was bigger than that."

"It was about us." Thalor's usually calm voice has an edge I've never heard before. "You took our technology. You stole a transport pod. You vanished."

"I did what I had to do." I try to sound firm, but my voice is already giving up on me.

Zegran's face is so close I can taste the heat of his breath. "Did you think of us at all?"

Of course I did. Every goddamn minute.

"Yes," I whisper. "More than you'll ever know."

Zegran's light patterns go dark, pulsing with tension. The expression on his face darkens, too.

"You belong to us," he snarls.

He rips at my clothes, and I gasp. My boobs hang out, heavy and bare. Does he plan for me to be naked in public when I re-board the Drayzok station?

"Zegran, wait—" I start, but I shut up when Korvan grabs me roughly from behind.

"We're going to remind you where you belong," he growls.

"We're still in the shuttle," I try again, weaker now. "You're not even gonna wait?"

Korvan's deep laugh vibrates against my skull. "You think you get to set the rules? After running? You belong to us. We'll take what's ours."

"I think she likes that idea," Thalor tells him.

He would know. He's shoved two of his fingers in my pussy, feeling exactly how slick I am.

"Her body already knows she's ours."

I close my eyes for a moment, trying not to remember what they do to the bodies in their hierarchy that step out of line.

But I can't let the question go unasked. "Are you going to punish me like you punished your warriors?"

I peek my eyes open when all movement around me halts.

"No," Zegran says when I meet his gaze. "This is not a punishment to deliver justice. It is punishment for reclaiming."

"You made us chase you across the stars," Thalor adds. "This is how a Drayzok man shows you he will fight for you. How we remind you of our connection."

Zegran asks, "Do you understand?"

Don't say yes. Don't say yes.

Maybe if I tell them I don't understand, I can get out of this. They'll find another way, a more human way, to express what they feel for me.

And I'll never get to experience the full fury and passion of my Drayzok warriors.

I want to know them. Want to feel them, all of them, for who they really are.

So I say it: "Yes. I understand."

I know what it means to them, my understanding.

I know it means they won't hold back now.

They pop my cuffs off, but only because they wanna restrain me using their own bodies.

Six huge hands, grabbing me and lifting me and slamming me against the cold metal wall. Korvan and Zegran grab my arms on each side and pin them to the wall, holding me there with such strength, I can't move away.

My legs dangle. That is, until Thalor hauls both my thighs up with one forearm to get to my pussy.

He spreads my folds open with his fingers. I know he could make me come almost instantly if he wanted to, so I know pleasure is not the point.

This is about opening me up and humiliating me.

"See how she drips for us," he says, making me wish I could snap my legs closed. "You've been needy and empty without us, haven't you, our little slut?"

My pussy clenches and I shut my eyes, knowing they can see it.

My eyes fly back open when Korvan speaks.

"We're gonna fuck that need right outta you."

"Punishment talk excites you," Zegran says, smirking. "Like the filthy little whore you are."

"Shut up," I mutter. My cheeks burn.

But I can't hide anything from them in this position.

"I wonder if she'll talk so bravely through the punishment itself?" Korvan looks at Zegran.

"We could begin and find out."

They haven't started yet?

Zegran dips his head, and Korvan quickly follows. On either side of me, they both bring their teeth to the delicate spot where my neck meets my shoulder.

Then they scrape their teeth along my skin, just enough to cut me.

I yelp, then groan as Thalor makes me feel pleasure in it, stroking my clit hard.

"You. Are. Ours."

They're all saying it, and I'm finding it impossible to argue.

This is not a good time to see Thalor pull out a new tech device. I have a feeling this little blue thing isn't one of the feel-good toys.

"What the hell is that?" I eye the device warily.

He grins. "It's not from hell. Just from my lab. Enhanced neural stimulator."

He presses it to my hip. There's a sting, then a wash of heat.

Suddenly, everything's too much. Everything I'm feeling, I'm feeling it all over my body.

The cold wall, their warm light patterns, Korvan's and Zegran's squeezing hands—all of it dialed up to eleven.

"What the fuck did you do?" I gasp, trembling.

"Jacked up your sensitivity," Thalor says. "So when we make you feel something..." He nods at Korvan, who clamps his teeth around my nipple. "You'll feel it everywhere."

"Fuck!" The pain is unbelievable, making me feel it all throughout my body.

But since my nipple feels good too, all I can do is throw my head back and tremble.

The shuttle's vibrations make me feel like I'm at the center of one big hum.

"Now your punishment has begun." Zegran's voice sounds booming, dark and triumphant. "And it won't stop until you forget every reason you ever had to leave."

God help me.

Korvan and Zegran let me down from the wall, only to grab me by the shoulders and force me down to my knees. When I drop to the metal floor, I feel the impact everywhere.

I'm face-to-crotch with Zegran now, right as he unfastens his uniform pants. Out pops his cock. I've been here before, but this time it feels different, with those lightning stripes throbbing with angry light.

Korvan comes down behind me while Thalor circles us, adjusting a control pad for that damn sensitivity device on me.

"Open," Zegran orders, wrapping his hand around my jaw.

He doesn't care that I'm trying to take a breath before I swallow his cock. His lights flash in irritation when I hesitate.

He grips my cheeks vice-tight and jerks his chin at Korvan behind me.

A sharp slap lands on my ass. Holy hell. Thalor's damn device sends the sensation all over my flesh.

I yelp, and Zegran immediately crams his cock between my lips.

He pushes deep immediately, scraping against my tongue with the ridges on his shaft. I choke, my eyes watering, but he's not in the mood to go easy.

"You will never run from us again," Zegran snarls. He fists my hair and keeps me right where he wants me, fucking my mouth like he means it. "Never."

Not like I could talk back even if I wanted. His cock fills my mouth, that metallic-sweet alien flavor pouring over my tastebuds. I have no choice but to let my throat open up.

With drool and tears dripping down my face, I don't know if humiliation is a sensation I can feel all over my body. But it sure feels like it. Like I'm flushing and feverish everywhere.

Korvan yanks my ass back. I feel the fat tip of his cock at my slit, already slick with the wetness dripping from me.

"It's like you said, Thalor. Her body knows who she belongs to."

He pushes in, his thickness punishing against my inner walls. He stretches me so wide, and with Thalor's device turned on, my whole body aches with fiery pleasure.

"We've got her where we want her." Thalor sets down his control pad, so I guess that means he's calibrated his little torture device like he wants it.

I've taken all three of them before. It's not that alone that makes my heart skip as he closes in.

It's the look on Thalor's face. It's a dark look, one that reminds me this isn't just an ordinary romp in the sack for these guys.

This is a reclaiming of what they thought they'd lost. And to the Drayzok, only brutality can accomplish that.

Korvan moves under me to make room for Thalor. Not that the new position makes him any less harsh as he fucks my pussy.

"Only one hole left," Thalor says, gripping my ass cheeks. "And I believe it requires the harshest punishment."

I go wide-eyed. This already feels pretty damn harsh, I can promise him that.

Only I couldn't tell him if I tried, not with Zegran's cock stuffing my mouth. I try to wriggle away, but it's useless—I'm pinned between Zegran's cock in my mouth and Korvan's monster dick in my pussy.

"Hold her," Thalor says, and Korvan tightens his grip on my hips until I can't even squirm. "I've calculated exactly how to make her feel immensely punished."

Thalor lines himself up behind me, slick fingers stretching my ass open. It feels like he's using some kind of lube, but it doesn't help much. His sensitivity device makes me feel the painful stretch all over my body.

As soon as the blunt head of his cock hits my tight ring of muscle, Thalor surges forward without hesitation. He pushes into my ass, burning and stretching me so intensely, I can hardly handle it.

But I have no choice but to handle it.

"You belong to us," Zegran reminds me again. "Every part of you."

Korvan and Thalor roar in agreement, fucking me harder.

I'm filled in every hole, but this isn't like the other times when they've fucked me all at once. There's no smooth synchronization, no teamwork to make me feel as good as possible.

They're each just taking what they want from me, trying to use me up and claim me as hard as possible.

It makes for a frenzied fucking. Zegran's fucking my mouth so hard I can barely breathe, ramming past my gag reflex without mercy.

Korvan's driving in from below, his cock splitting me open with every lunge. Thalor's drilling into my ass and making my whole body feel it.

They're tossing me around like a rag doll. All my weight means nothing to them as they lift and push and pound me.

When Korvan jerks me back on his cock, Zegran slips from my mouth. Zegran growls and yanks me to shove himself back in, which leads Thalor to bury himself even deeper in my ass to make sure he doesn't lose his spot.

It's chaos. Pure, punishing chaos. Even without the extra sensitivity device, this would be the most intense mix of sensations I've ever felt.

The worst part? I'm actually about to get off on it. I can feel my orgasm rising.

And I'm terrified—because what if they don't even let me come? What if this is part of my punishment, bringing me to the edge of an explosive release and not letting it happen?

I scream as both Korvan and Thalor come down hard at the same time, drilling deep into my pussy and ass. Much to Zegran's frustration, my mouth jerks free of his cock again.

"I'm scared!" I manage to shout just before he puts his cock back in.

He pauses. "Good. You should be."

"No," I pant. "I'm scared you're not going to let me orgasm."

A dark grin spreads across Zegran's face. He looks over my head at the others.

"Did you hear that? Our little runaway is afraid we won't let her release." His eyes lock on mine with wicked intent. "Korvan. Thalor. Let's make her orgasm."

My heart flutters with relief—until he keeps talking.

"Not once. Not twice. Make her orgasm until she can't take it anymore. And then do it again."

I shake my head, panic spiking, but Zegran shoves himself back in my mouth and laughs as I choke on him.

Korvan slides his hand to my clit. He knows exactly what to do with it, and now I regret every moan that helped him learn. He rolls my bud perfectly between his thick fingers.

Thanks to Thalor's sensitivity device, my whole body feels like it's on the edge of something. As if Korvan and Zegran are rubbing my clit too, even though Korvan's cock is rocking in my ass and Zegran's is sliding down my throat.

I couldn't fight it if I tried. I close my eyes and let the orgasm come.

And I feel it all. Everywhere. Not just the incredible pleasure of the orgasm, but the battering ram that is Korvan's cock in my pussy, and the control Zegran has over my whole head, and the deep, invasive sensation of Thalor in my ass.

It's so all-consuming, it goes beyond just what I feel. This is who I *am*.

I am the whimper in my throat. The tightening of my toes. The thrill of being owned.

I wouldn't be me without this.

"Again," Zegran orders.

I'm so sensitive to noise, his voice sounds like it's booming in my head. It doesn't take much for them to trigger another orgasm, and another, and more after that, until I feel like I'm floating, shaking and sobbing between them.

They don't slow down. Thalor and Korvan keep fucking my ass and my pussy when Zegran finally comes.

His cock jerks hard, flooding my mouth. He doesn't let me go, holding my face against him and forcing me to swallow it all.

Korvan makes me orgasm again before Zegran is finished, and I choke, sending Zegran's jizz dribbling down my chin.

When he pulls out, Zegran spurts again and paints my tits with his tingling cum, making me feel tingles everywhere. When he rubs it in and pinches my nipples hard, another orgasm overtakes the last one, making me scream.

"I can't—please—too much," I sob.

But Korvan and Thalor still have to finish.

While they keep fucking me, Zegran smacks my breasts, sending them heaving in one direction, and then another. He's never been this rough with me before, and in my sensitive state, that alone is enough to make me want to come.

"Now that your mouth is free, you can tell us who you belong to," he says. "Keep saying it until we're finished with you."

I don't even think about trying to defy him.

"I'm yours! Zegran. Thalor. Korvan. I belong to you."

Korvan and Thalor both roar, and I can tell they're about to come. I keep saying what they want to hear. I have to say it between sobs and gasps, but I use all my strength to keep saying it.

It feels so fucking good when they fill me up, I almost forget this is punishment. The sensation of satisfaction fills me from my toes to my head.

What reminds me this is punishment? That would be the part where they shove me down, come on my ass and then spank me, smacking hard to rub the whole wet mess in.

I think maybe it's over. But then Korvan pinches my nipples while Thalor presses my clit, just to make me orgasm again... and again... and again...

And I think maybe I'll feel like this forever.

***

I wake up to movement, and that's when I realize my trio made me come until I passed out.

Those fuckers. Those crazy fuckers made me feel more plea-sure-pain than I ever have in my life, and called that "punishment."

And those fuckers are all mine.

My chest feels warm.

Someone's carrying me. Everything hurts, but there's a strange peace settling over me, like I survived something big and made it to the other side.

I crack my eyes open and Zegran's looking down at me. His fury's gone. His face looks tender.

"She's awake," he says.

Then Thalor's wiping my face, as gently as Zegran cradles me.

"Where..." My voice is hoarse.

"We've docked with the space station," Thalor answers. "We're taking you back to our quarters."

I look around and see Korvan's guarding the door, making sure no one else gets a peek at me in my naked state.

As we move through the ship toward their quarters—our quarters, I suppose—I nestle closer to Zegran's chest. His spines are retracted now, his skin cool and soothing. I let myself sink into it.

They'll say they reclaimed me to keep me from running away again, but I don't want to run anymore. I don't want to leave them.

I want to belong to them. To these brutal bastards who just wrecked me completely.

In our quarters, Zegran tries to lay me down in my private room, but I don't want to be here.

"I want to be with you," I insist.

Korvan smirks down at me. "What makes you think we're going anywhere?"

All three of them crowd the bed to settle in around me.

He's right. I don't need to worry. There's no question of this.

I'm theirs.

CHAPTER 24

THALOR

I check the diagnostic readings on my wrist interface for the fifth time in as many minutes, tracking Rylak's location through the station's neural network.

The green dot pulses steadily. He's in the tech temple, which makes sense. Where else would a guilt-ridden technician go but to the sacred space where our ancestors' wisdom still echoes through circuit and crystal?

My skin patterns flicker with agitation as I navigate the curved corridors of the station. It's been a week since Quinn returned with us. We're rebuilding what her escape to Earth shattered.

And my mind keeps circling back to the larger problem she's exposed.

The tech temple is where I'll find Rylak, but will I find answers?

I head toward the transport tubes. Off-duty warriors step aside as I pass, some nodding in recognition, others averting their eyes.

Word has traveled quickly. Everyone knows about the human female who escaped and was recaptured. Between this and the dining hall incident, Quinn's earning herself quite the reputation.

I reach a transport tube and step inside, keying in the sequence for the temple level. The tube hums to life, propelling me downward through the station's superstructure.

As the light panels flash past, I remember Quinn's face when she first saw this technology. The wonder in her dark eyes, the questions tumbling from her lips faster than I could answer them.

She's so much more than our manuals claimed she would be.

The transport tube slows, then stops with a soft chime. I exit into the dim blue lighting of the temple level, my skin patterns automatically adjusting to glow brighter in response.

I turn down the ornate archway leading to the tech temple, my mind still churning over the problem.

The original fury we felt at Quinn's escape has transformed into something more complex.

Because she was right. If what she says is true—and I have no reason to doubt her now—then thousands of human females are being kept in a state that amounts to captivity, not proper mating. They're unable to communicate their needs or understand what's happening to them.

Just like Quinn was, before the translator chip.

I remember the day I first showed her my technological innovations for pleasure enhancement. It was after we'd given her the chip, when she'd begun to relax around us.

She was never shy, that's for sure.

"So what's this one do?" she'd asked, pointing to the neural interface bands I'd left on my workbench.

My skin patterns pulsed with excitement. Never had I expected to have a human female mate I could share technology information with. The idea was once so far-fetched, I'd never even dreamed of it.

But the reality of it is quite a dream indeed.

"It's a sensory amplification system," I explained, picking up the sleek metallic bands. "When worn by partners during mating, it creates a feedback loop of sensation. What one feels, the other experiences as well."

Quinn's eyes widened, a flush creeping up her neck. "So if you... and I... then you'd feel what I feel?"

"And you would feel what I feel," I confirmed, watching her expression carefully. "The experience becomes shared. Intensified."

She reached out to touch the bands, tracing the intricate circuitry embedded in the metal. "Did you invent this?"

Pride surged through me. She must think highly of my skills to ask such a question.

"I improved upon existing technology. The original designs were crude, unbalanced. They favored the male experience. I recalibrated them to create true reciprocity."

"That's... impressive," she said, and the simple praise affected me more deeply than any technical commendation I've ever received.

"Would you like to try them?" I asked.

We both laughed then, realizing I hadn't even gotten the question out before she was already trying to fit the bands on her wrists.

I wish she could see the tech temple. She'd likely appreciate the significance of it.

Maybe someday I will bring her here. Where the doors are etched with the circuit patterns of our ancestors' first great innovations.

The neural interface, the gravity manipulation field, the interstellar drive. All gifts that transformed us from planetary dwellers to masters of the stars.

I press my palm against the entrance panel, and the doors slide open with a whisper of perfectly calibrated hydraulics. Inside, the temple soars upward, its walls lined with holographic displays of our technological evolution.

The central altar is a masterpiece of engineering—a floating platform of interlocked metals that shift and reconfigure continuously, representing the ever-evolving nature of knowledge.

And there, kneeling before it, is Rylak.

His smaller frame is hunched forward, eyes closed in meditation. The technician's uniform he wears gleams with the embedded status symbols of his rank. Even among his class, Rylak holds elevated status.

I approach slowly, respecting the sacred space. The tech temple is where we Drayzok come to honor the ancestors who gifted us with our foundational knowledge. It is where we give thanks for the technology that shapes our existence.

And where we seek forgiveness when we misuse that gift.

Rylak's eyes snap open as I draw near.

"I knew you would find me again eventually," he says, not bothering to rise from his kneeling position. "Once again, your persistence is predictable."

"I need to speak with you." I stop a respectful distance from the altar.

"And I need to commune with the ancestors. Some of us take our duties seriously, Thalor."

I bite back a sharp response. Antagonizing him won't help.

"What brings you to the temple, Rylak? It's not your scheduled devotion time."

He narrows his eyes. "I'm seeking forgiveness for a grave transgression. For allowing myself to be coerced into violating the sacred protocols regarding human females." His gaze hardens. "By you and your trio."

"You mean the translator chip." I step closer, lowering my voice. "The one that proved our understanding of human females has been fundamentally flawed."

Rylak scoffs, finally rising to his feet. He's still shorter than me, but in this sacred space, his technician status grants him authority I lack.

"What it proved is that your trio's obsession with your human pet has clouded your judgment. The protocols exist for a reason."

"And what if that reason is based on a lie?" I counter. "We've spoken with our mate. Quinn. We've listened to her. She's not some sex-crazed lesser being, Rylak. None of them are."

"You've spoken with her," he repeats. "And I suppose she's convinced you she's the intellectual equal of a Drayzok? Are you sure she didn't put you under a spell with her gibberish?"

I clench my fists. "She's demonstrated intelligence, creativity, and adaptation that contradict everything our manuals told us to expect. She can operate our technology, understand complex concepts, engage in philosophical debate—"

"One anomaly doesn't invalidate established knowledge," Rylak interrupts. "Perhaps your human is unusual. Or perhaps you're seeing what you want to see to justify your unnatural attachment to her."

"Meet her," I challenge. "Speak with her yourself. Test her understanding of our technology. I've been teaching her, and she learns with remarkable speed."

Rylak's posture stiffens. "I want nothing to do with your translator-chipped human female. The very existence of such an aberration is an offense against the natural order."

"The natural order?" I step closer, my patience wearing thin. "Or just the order that benefits those in power? Think, Rylak. What if the Original Agents lied to us about human females? What if they deliberately misrepresented their capabilities to maintain control of the exchange?"

"Speculation without evidence," he dismisses, though I catch a flicker of uncertainty in his patterns.

"I have evidence. Quinn is my evidence. And if one human female is more than we were told, then logically, others must be as well." I press my advantage. "Your word carries weight, Rylak. As a technician, your assessment could validate these findings. We need to reconsider the prohibition against translator chips for human females."

Rylak's laugh is sharp. "You want me to go to the authorities and suggest they're perpetuating a scheme against human females? That the one chance we have to mate and breed in the absence of our own females is based on a falsehood?" He shakes his head. "I would be stripped of my rank, or worse."

"Your rank matters." It makes me grit my teeth to remind him of the power he holds. "No one can dismiss your honorable status."

He lifts his chest. "Perhaps you overestimate the influence of my position, warrior. Your trio unit is also highly ranked, and I don't see you three risking your lives or status to convince the authorities of your human's intelligence."

The accusation stings, because it's true. Despite Quinn pleading with us—despite her even leaving us to try to save her people—we have not spoken up for her. Because of the risk.

Rylak drops his voice to a hiss. "You threatened my safety to get that chip. Now you want me to risk what remains of my career on your human's claims?"

"I'm not asking you to take action today," I say, recalibrating my approach and stepping back. "Just to think on the possibility that we've been wrong. That perhaps, the reason translator chips are forbidden to human females is to keep them from telling us the truth."

Rylak turns away, his attention returning to the altar. "Leave me, Thalor. I have prayers to complete."

I know when to pause a battle for another day. Pushing further will only strengthen his resistance. I turn to go, frustration crackling through my patterns.

"There is another option," Rylak calls after me.

I pause, looking back over my shoulder.

"If you truly believe this matter is of such importance, take it to the Command Council directly. Your trio has the status to request an audience. Let them judge whether your human's claims merit investigation."

The Command Council. The highest authority on the ship, representatives of the governing body that rules all Drayzok territories.

To approach them with such a radical challenge to established protocols would be horrendously dangerous.

Potentially catastrophic for our careers, our status, and perhaps even our lives, if they deemed it severe enough heresy.

But what's the alternative? Continue as we are, knowing what we know? Watch Quinn's trust in us erode as she realizes we won't fight for others like her? Lose her again, this time perhaps for good?

Rylak has already turned away, dismissing me. But his suggestion burns in my mind as I exit the temple.

The Command Council.

If we take this step, what would we unleash?

Chapter 25

Quinn

"There's no precedent for this."

I'm pretty sure I've thoroughly worn out Korvan and Zegran with this debate, and only Thalor's still standing.

That's fine. I'll get him, too. He's a sucker for a good intellectual challenge.

"Like we've never done anything without precedent before?" I sweep my arms out. "Look where we are right now."

My trio's parked around me on the edge of our sleeping platform. They converted one of the rooms in their quarters into this, our shared bedroom. I still have my own room if I want privacy, but they'd decided it felt too much like I was still a captive when we didn't have a shared space.

"The Command Council rarely grants audiences to warrior-class petitioners," Thalor says. "It's already unusual enough that we're bringing this to them ourselves. But a human challenging them? A human female, at that? They won't have it."

"I don't care if it shocks them to see me there." I sniff. "Let them be shocked! I want to go with you."

"Absolutely not," Zegran says, for the third or fourth time tonight. That authoritative rumble in his voice used to make my blood run cold. Now it just makes me want to dig in my heels.

"Why not? I'm the evidence. I'm the proof that everything they believe about human women is bullshit."

Thalor shakes his head, his patterns dimming. "The Council chamber is no place for a human female. There will be hundreds of Drayzok males present, many of whom have never acquired a mate. The risk is—"

"I've been in danger before," I cut him off. "I've faced down Rust Rats with nothing but a homemade slingshot. I'll take my chances with your people, especially with you three with me."

Korvan's hand swallows mine up. "It's not the same, Quinn. Council hearings are formal proceedings, following protocols established centuries ago. Humans aren't part of those protocols."

"That's exactly my point," I pull my hand free. "Humans aren't part of your protocols because you don't see us as equals. You've never let us speak for ourselves."

Zegran rises to his feet. "The Council chamber will be filled with unmated warriors. You've seen what happened in the dining hall during your escape attempt. If even one loses control..."

"They can sense I'm claimed now, right? You told me that's what happens when you mark me. Besides, you'll all be right next to me. No one's going to try anything again after what you did to the last guys who tried."

"And you were disturbed by what we did to them," Thalor says quietly. "You may be disturbed by what you see here, as well. The Council procedures aren't what you're used to. One misstep could invalidate our entire petition."

"So teach me. Right now." I plant my hands on my hips. "I'm a quick study, remember? You said so yourself."

Korvan says, "This isn't about your intelligence. It's about your safety."

"No, it's about control," I snap back. "You want to protect me? Fine. But don't hide me away like I'm something shameful or fragile." I take a deep breath, trying to steady my voice. "If you're serious about changing how your people treat human women, then let me show them what we really are. Let me speak for myself."

A heavy silence falls. They exchange glances.

"She has a point," Thalor finally says. "Her presence would be powerful evidence. The Council would have to acknowledge her intelligence if she addresses them directly."

Korvan huffs. "Or they could see it as an insult to tradition. Having a human female speak in the sacred chamber, it's..."

"It's a risk," Zegran agrees, his gaze still fixed on me. "But then, this entire petition is a risk."

"I need to be there," I insist, stepping closer to him. Despite everything, despite knowing what these men are capable of when they're challenged, I'm not backing down. "How can you argue that human women deserve voices if you won't let me use mine?"

Zegran lets out a long, slow exhale.

"If you come with us," he says slowly, "you will need to follow our lead exactly. One word out of place, one action that could be interpreted as disrespect, and we may not be able to control what happens next."

"I'll be the perfect mate," I promise. "Respectful, attentive, and completely capable of blowing their minds when they realize I can string a coherent sentence together."

Thalor's lips twitch into a reluctant smile. "We would need to prepare you. Teach you the formal greetings, the proper responses."

"Fine. Let's start now."

***

The Council chamber is nothing like I imagined. I expected something metal and functional, like most of the Drayzok spaces I've seen.

Instead, I step into what feels like an ancient cathedral. Soaring ceilings disappear into darkness above us.

The columns lining the aisle are made of black glass that glows from inside, like frozen lightning. The wall etchings remind me of the light patterns on Drayzok skin, only brighter.

There are hundreds of Drayzok in here. All male, all packed into the rising tiers around us, their skin creating a living, shifting light show.

It's beautiful, and also terrifying. So much power aimed at the center of this room.

My throat closes. If this goes bad, I'll be ripped apart before I can even scream.

Zegran's hand settles on the small of my back, steady and warm.

"Stay close," he murmurs.

I nod, grateful for his touch. Korvan flanks my right, Thalor on my left. They form a wall around me as we head down the central aisle.

Heads turn as we pass, Drayzok faces turning to watch us. The crowd buzzes with voices.

They all know why we're here today. I catch enough of their words to tell me that.

"She's that female."

"Translator chip."

"Warriors' petition."

Some of them sound curious. Some sound hostile. None of it's friendly.

I keep my chin up, my gaze fixed on the raised dais at the far end of the chamber, where five Drayzok sit on ornate chairs.

The Command Council.

They look older than most Drayzok I've seen, their spines dulled with age, skin so dark blue, it's almost purple. Their robes are elaborate, covered in symbols and shiny stuff for ranks I can't begin to decipher.

Despite everything—the danger, the crowd, the stares—I feel proud walking beside my trio. They're risking everything to change their society. For me. For women like me.

They told me they've never done anything like this before, and they never could've imagined it before me. But here they are now.

My brave-ass warriors.

We reach a glowing circle at the center of the room. Zegran guides me to sit between them, not quite hidden, but not quite center stage.

"Remember," Thalor whispers, "don't speak until the Council acknowledges you directly."

I nod, inhaling deeply. We went over this a dozen times in our quarters, but the reality of standing in front of hundreds of Drayzok males is way more intimidating than I expected.

Guess I should stop being surprised by the strength of these brutes.

Thalor leans over again. "The technician is here. Three tiers up, near the service entrance."

I look where he flicks his chin. I guess that's Rylak, sitting stiffly with other technicians. Their uniforms are fancier, glowing like circuit boards. Rylak meets my eye and looks away fast.

My trio told me how they "convinced" him to hand over my translator chip. Threats. Intimidation. I should probably feel bad, but honestly, they gave me a voice, so I can't quite bring myself to condemn my guys for it.

A deep voice resonates through the chamber. Every Drayzok instantly shuts up. The central Council member rises, his robes flowing around him like liquid shadow.

"Warriors of the seventh battalion," he intones. "You have request-ed this audience to address matters of the human mating protocols. State your purpose."

Zegran steps up, performing their formal salute: right fist to op-posite shoulder, head inclined just enough to show respect, but not surrender.

"Honored Council, we come before you with evidence that chal-lenges our understanding of human females. We believe the Origi-nal Agents provided false information about human females' nature, intelligence, and mating preferences. This misinformation has led to practices that are..." he hesitates, choosing his words carefully, "...in-efficient. And potentially detrimental to successful mating bonds."

Inefficient. Not cruel or wrong. Just inefficient. We agreed on this approach. Framing everything in terms the Drayzok leadership would value.

A different Council member leans forward, eyes narrow. "You base these claims on what evidence, warrior?"

Thalor steps forward now. "Our human female mate has demon-strated intelligence, linguistic ability, and technological aptitude far beyond what the manuals indicate is possible. With access to a trans-lator chip, she has communicated complex thoughts, learned our sys-tems, and integrated successfully into our trio."

A ripple of murmurs spreads through the crowd.

Another Council member speaks, voice dripping with disdain. "Human females are breeding stock, warriors. Their purpose is re-production and physical release. The Original Agents made this clear. Your attachment to your pet is clouding your judgment."

Pet? I bite my tongue, remembering my promise to stay silent until I'm directly addressed.

"They lack the neural complexity for higher thought," continues the Council member. "Their resistance to mating is instinctual, not rational. A primitive biological response that enhances male pleasure through conquest. This is why the fral'ra process is necessary. The manuals are explicit on this point."

Korvan's lights go almost black with anger, but his words are clipped, contained. "With respect, Council Member Poltar, we have found these assertions to be incorrect. Our mate has demonstrated—"

"Your mate, warrior," interrupts another Council member, "is property. A resource allocated to your trio for reproduction and comfort. That you find her amusing or believe she has intelligence speaks to your lack of proper perspective, not to any quality in the human."

My hands curl into fists, nails digging in.

The central Council guy raises a hand, silencing the rest. "You claim to have provided this human female with a translator chip. This is a direct violation of established protocols."

"Yes," Zegran admits without hesitation. "We did. And that violation revealed the truth—that human females are intelligent beings capable of complex thought and communication."

"The prohibition exists for a reason, warrior," says the oldest-looking Council member, speaking for the first time. "Translator technology is sophisticated. It can create the illusion of intelligence where none exists, translating basic animal responses into seemingly coherent language."

That's it. I can't take it anymore. My head snaps up, and I step forward.

"That's not true."

The chamber falls deadly silent. Hundreds of Drayzok freeze, all eyes turning to me. I feel Zegran tense beside me, but he doesn't pull me back.

The Council members stare down at me, their expressions ranging from shock to outrage to cold curiosity.

"The human female speaks," says the central member.

"Yes." Skipping the salute I'm supposed to do, I keep talking. "I do speak. I also think. I feel. I understand. And I'm standing right here while you talk about me like I'm some kind of farm animal."

Thalor slides his hand into mine, squeezing just enough to ground me.

The central Council member studies me for a beat, then inclines his head slightly. "Very well. Since your warriors have brought you here to demonstrate your supposed intelligence, you may address the Council directly."

Time to go for it. My palms are sweaty, but my voice is clear.

"My name is Quinn Morgyn," I say, as loud as I can. "Before I was taken by the Drayzok, I was a survivor on Earth. I scavenged, I traded, I protected myself and others. I was a person with my own thoughts and dreams, and I made my own choices."

I look around the chamber, daring anyone to look away. "The Original Agents lied to you. They told you human women are only good for sex and breeding. They told you we like being forced, that our resistance is just a game. Those were lies told by men who wanted to exploit both your people and mine."

The Council members' light patterns flicker, but no one interrupts.

"When I was first captured, I couldn't understand what was happening to me. I couldn't communicate. I was terrified. The fral'ra process you subject women to, it's terrifying. Being held down, being touched and denied release over and over. We can enjoy sex. Some of us even like rough, dominating sex, like you like it..."

I gulp, not sure how much to share about that side of myself. I change course and gesture toward my trio.

"These three gave me a translation chip. They let me speak. They listened when I told them what was wrong. And everything changed between us. I'm not saying I love being abducted from my home planet, but I've found a way to adapt, even to find happiness, because I'm treated like I'm more than some mindless animal."

I look back at the Council, not blinking. "Other women deserve the same chance. They deserve to understand what's happening to them. They deserve to be heard. If you truly want successful mating bonds between Drayzok and humans, then give human women your translation chips. Let us speak. Let us be your partners, not your livestock."

I finish and step back, suddenly aware of how still the chamber has become. No whispers, no movement. Just hundreds of eyes fixed on me with serious expressions.

The Council members glance at each other. Their patterns flash, but their faces are stone.

No deliberation, no discussion. They already know what they're going to say.

My heart sinks.

The central member faces us again. "The Council has heard your petition. We find no compelling evidence to warrant changes to the established human mating protocols. The prohibition against translator chips for human females will remain in effect."

Just like that. All my words, all the hope? Gone.

"But—" I start.

Zegran's hand on my arm stops me. His grip is firm, a clear warning. It's time to shut up.

"The Council's decision is final," continues the central member. "This audience is concluded. Warriors, return to your duties. And ensure your human female understands her proper place."

The tone sounds again, signaling the end of the hearing. All around us, Drayzok stand up, the noise of conversation swelling.

Zegran hustles me out, Korvan and Thalor close behind. It's not until we're alone in a side corridor that we stop.

The weight of defeat sits heavy on my shoulders. I thought—we all thought—that the truth could be enough. That once the Council heard me speak, saw my reason, they would have to face reality.

We were wrong.

"They didn't even pretend to consider it," Thalor says. "Not even a token deliberation."

Korvan slams his hand against the wall. "They weren't surprised. Not by her intelligence, not by her speech. Not surprised at all."

Zegran's face goes cold. "Because they already knew."

We all go still.

"They know human women aren't what the manuals claim," Thalor says slowly. "They know the Original Agents lied."

"And they're keeping up with those lies anyway," I finish. "But why?"

"That's what we need to find out," Zegran says.

"And we will," Korvan promises. "Whatever it takes."

I look at them, my three alien warriors who started as my captors and somehow became my champions. Something's happening here, and we're stepping right into the middle of it.

The Council isn't just misguided. They're deliberately perpetuating a system they know is wrong.

And I believe my warriors when they say they're going to find out why.

CHAPTER 26

ZEGRAN

The private Council chamber feels like a trap. Too small, too quiet, the air too still.

My skin patterns flicker with agitation as we enter, Quinn's smaller form half-hidden behind my bulk.

I sense Korvan's tension to my right. He's nearly vibrating with contained aggression. Thalor moves with measured steps on my left, his mind probably churning with calculations and ideas.

The two Council members wait for us. Threg, with his upright diplomatic posture, and Poltar, with his cold, assessing gaze.

I can tell they're irritated by our request to confer with them privately, but we have to try. For Quinn. For all those like her.

Besides, their level of irritation is nothing compared to ours.

Threg gestures toward the seating arrangement. Four chairs for us, positioned lower than their elevated perches. A deliberate power move.

"Iron Guardian Zegran. Keepers Thalor and Korvan." Threg's voice carries the practiced neutrality of a career politician. He doesn't acknowledge Quinn's presence at all.

I perform the formal salute, careful to show respect without subservience. "Council members. We appreciate this private audience."

"Granted at great inconvenience," Poltar says, his voice rough with impatience. "The public hearing was not sufficient?"

"The public hearing was a farce." I keep my tone level despite the anger pulsing beneath my skin. "We were not permitted a full deliberation for our case."

Quinn steps out from behind me. Her chin's lifted in that defiant way that once gave me the urge to break her. Now, it fills me with pride.

"You mean they dismissed what I had to say," she says.

Threg finally looks at her. "The human female. Yes."

"Her name is Quinn." My spines extend slightly as I correct him.

Poltar waves a hand. "Her name is irrelevant."

I'm severely tempted to make sure he remembers her name by letting Quinn demonstrate her combat skills on him, but Threg interrupts.

"The prohibition against translator technology for human females is absolute. This matter has been settled."

Quinn steps forward, her soft body brushing against my arm.

"You wouldn't be so dismissive if you got to know the women you're condemning," she says. "Women like Katarina."

"Katarina?" Poltar pronounces Quinn's friend's name like it's the name of an invasive tech bug.

"A woman I knew on Earth," Quinn says. "She worked at a trading post run by a friend of mine. Quiet, smart, good with numbers. She could calculate values and exchange rates in her head faster than anyone I've ever met."

I watch the Council members' faces as Quinn speaks, searching for any sign of empathy or understanding. Threg maintains his diplomatic mask, but something in Poltar's expression makes my patterns darken with unease.

"Katarina wasn't a fighter like me," Quinn says. "She was gentle. Shy. When the Rust Rats took her to your people, she probably didn't even fight them. She wouldn't have known how."

"What relevance does this human's story have to our discussion?" Poltar says.

Quinn gives him a hard look, the fury of which he surely underestimates. "She's not just 'this human.' She had a life. And now she's probably strapped to a table somewhere on this station, terrified out of her mind because she has no idea what the hell you're trying to accomplish with your fral'ra process."

"The fral'ra process is a necessary step in preparing human females for mating," Threg recites, as if reading from one of the manuals. "It ensures—"

"It's torture," Quinn snaps. "You're torturing women because you won't let them understand what's happening."

I place a steadying hand on Quinn's shoulder, feeling the tension thrumming through her.

"All we ask is that the Council reconsider the prohibition against translator chips," I say. "Let human females communicate. Let us all understand each other."

Threg and Poltar exchange a glance. I've seen that look in the Council chamber—just before their instant rejection of our public petition.

"The prohibition stands," Threg says. "The social order must be maintained."

Something's wrong here. Their resistance feels too practiced, too absolute. I study their faces more carefully, trying to read past the formal expressions.

Threg sits with the rigidity of duty, his patterns pulsing in the measured rhythm of someone following orders. But Poltar...

Poltar's eyes keep drifting to Quinn, lingering on the curves of her body. There's something in his stare that makes my blood run cold. He's not merely dismissing her.

He desires her.

I move, positioning my body between Poltar's leering gaze and Quinn. My spines extend fully now, a clear dominance display that would be considered a breach of protocol in this formal setting.

"Is there a problem, Iron Guardian?" Poltar asks, his tone mocking.

"You haven't heard a word we've said," I growl. "This isn't about social order or protocols. This is about something else entirely."

Quinn steps to my side, refusing to be sheltered. She studies Poltar with her sharp eyes, recognition dawning on her face.

"I know that look," she says suddenly. "I've seen it on Earth. On spineless men who liked it when women were afraid."

Poltar's patterns flicker briefly before settling into a darker rhythm.

"You like things the way they are," Quinn continues, her voice hardening. "You don't want us to have translation chips because you like torturing us like this."

Nobody speaks. Threg shifts uncomfortably, but Poltar's expression remains unmoved. Unashamed.

"Is that true?" I demand, barely controlling the rage building in my chest.

Poltar leans back in his seat, looking relaxed despite the tension crackling through the room. "Your human is perceptive. Unusual."

"Answer the question," Korvan says from behind me.

"Very well." Poltar's mouth contorts into a cruel smile. "Yes. I prefer human females as they are... struggling. Their fear, their helplessness, these things are quite stimulating."

Quinn flinches beside me. "You sick bastard."

"It is our right," Poltar says, unperturbed by her disgust. "We are Drayzok. The dominant species. We require mates, and the females of our kind have turned from us. Why should we not take what we need from a lesser species?"

"Humans aren't lesser," Thalor argues. "They may be different, but they're equally capable and intelligent."

Poltar laughs, and it grates against my eardrums.

"An opinion not shared by many in our leadership, I assure you." He looks at me. "You should know, Iron Guardian, that you and your trio are not the norm. Many Drayzok males share my preference. Many enjoy the process of breaking an unwilling female."

I grit my teeth. "You must be stopped."

Poltar shakes his head. "There are enough of us in leadership to ensure your petition will never succeed. Enough to maintain the current protocols regardless of your evidence."

Threg clears his throat. "Poltar, perhaps we shouldn't—"

"No. Let them understand the futility of their position." Poltar leans forward, his patterns growing brighter with excitement. "Even now, transport ships carry fresh human females back to Draxith. Two months' journey, during which they will be properly prepared for their new roles. By the time they arrive, the practice will be firmly established on our homeworld as well."

Quinn's hand finds mine, gripping with surprising strength. "You're talking about thousands of women."

"Tens of thousands, eventually," Poltar confirms. "An efficient solution to our mating crisis."

"This isn't what the Drayzok stand for." I'm struggling to keep my voice level. "We are warriors, not predators. Once others know the truth..."

"Plenty already know," Poltar says smugly. "Those who matter have chosen their position. And you would be wise to accept yours. Unless you wish to face the consequences of continued defiance."

I step closer to his elevated seat, my height nearly bringing us eye to eye despite his raised position.

"Are you threatening us, Council Member?"

"Merely reminding you of political realities. I hold considerable influence in the Command hierarchy. Your trio's status, while impressive for the warrior class, is ultimately insignificant compared to mine."

I move closer, letting him appreciate the height of my fully extended spines. "And I am reminding you of physical realities. Your political power means nothing if your throat is crushed."

Threg rises abruptly. "This audience is concluded. Iron Guardian, such threats against a Council member could be considered treason."

Thalor counters, "And what would we consider the deliberate enslavement and violation of intelligent beings?"

I pull back, forcing my spines to retract slightly. I'll pull them out again when it matters. Fighting these two today won't win the battle.

"We're done here," I say to my trio. "For now."

Quinn's face is pale as we exit the chamber. But she walks with her head high.

Still, I can spot the slight tremor in her hands. The revelation that Drayzok males like Poltar actively enjoy attacking human females has shaken her more deeply than she wants to show.

Suddenly, our position in the corridor outside feels much too exposed. Warriors and technicians move past us, going about their duties. Some nod respectfully in my direction. Others glance curiously at Quinn.

I study their faces with new suspicion. How many share Poltar's preference? How many look at Quinn and see not a sentient being, but a toy whose fear is part of the game?

Korvan moves closer to Quinn's other side, creating a protective wall. Thalor takes position behind her, scanning for threats. Without discussing it, we've built a defensive formation around our mate.

"Everyone's staring," Quinn murmurs.

"Let them," Korvan growls. "Anyone tries to touch you, they lose the hand."

We make our way back to our residential unit in tense silence. Each passing warrior, each curious glance makes my patterns pulse with protective aggression. The walk that normally takes minutes feels like hours.

When the door finally slides closed behind us, sealing us into the safety of our quarters, Quinn's composure crumbles.

Her shoulders slump, her head drops, and her wail rips at something deep in my chest.

"We can't stop them, can we?" Her voice breaks. "All those women. Out there on those ships." Tears fill her eyes and spill down her cheeks. "I got lucky. I got you three. But the others..."

She covers her face with her hands, her body shaking with silent sobs. If I still believed what the manuals told me, I might try to pull her against me, claim her mouth with mine, and drive away her sadness with my cock.

But I know better now.

I pull her into my arms, holding her gently against my chest. I don't try to silence her crying or distract her from her pain. I just hold her, letting her feel whatever she needs to feel.

Thalor approaches, resting his hand on her back. His patterns shift to a soothing rhythm, gentle pulses of light to help slow her breathing.

Korvan joins us, encircling all three of us with his arms. His usual aggression is tempered now, his strength becoming a shelter rather than a weapon.

"We're not giving up," I promise against Quinn's hair. "We'll find a way."

Her tears soak into my chest as she clings to me. I hold her tighter, trying to convey with touch what words can't express.

I don't know how we'll fight this. I don't know if we can win against the entrenched power of men like Poltar.

But I know we have to keep trying. Giving up is not an option.

CHAPTER 27

QUINN

I wake up cocooned in blue flesh, three massive bodies curved around my softer form.

Zegran's arm drapes heavy across my waist, his normally flared spines retracted in sleep. Thalor's breath tickles my neck in steady, measured intervals. Behind me, Korvan's massive chest rises and falls, rumbling with something between a snore and a purr.

The memories of last night's tears sting fresh. Council members dismissing thousands of women as playthings. The revelation that some Drayzok actually prefer to see our terror.

But here, surrounded by my trio, the horror feels somehow distant. Manageable.

I must have fallen asleep crying. Fuck, I really do hate crying in front of people. But I didn't even get to think about that last night. I just let go, and they let me.

Last thing I remember is Zegran holding me while Korvan and Thalor formed a wall around us both.

The early station cycle casts a dim blue glow across our sleeping platform. I study their faces. They're so damn dear to me now.

Zegran's fierce features are softened in sleep, his hard eyes relaxed. Thalor's analytical brain is finally quiet, eyes closed, long lashes brushing his midnight-blue cheeks. Korvan's permanent scowl is smoothed out, making him look almost gentle despite his massive bulk.

My gaze travels lower, over the expanse of their bodies.

Light patterns pulse slowly beneath their skin in sleep rhythms. Zegran's lightning-bolt markings zigzag down his torso toward the thick ridge of his cock, half-hard even in slumber. Thalor's geometric patterns create a hypnotic dance across his leaner frame. Korvan's swirling circles illuminate his powerful muscles, dipping into the valleys between each defined ridge.

Damn, they're sexy.

Heat pools between my thighs, my body responding on instinct. I never wanted sex this often before them. On Earth, getting laid was pretty low on my survival priority list—somewhere between finding matching socks and alphabetizing my canned goods.

Now I wake up dripping wet, my skin hungry for their touch.

I shift closer to Zegran, pressing my lips against his. His reaction is immediate, eyes snapping open, patterns brightening. He slides his hand between my legs without hesitation, fingers finding my clit expertly.

"Good morning to you too," I whisper against his mouth.

His grunt is neither confirmation nor denial, just pure male satisfaction as his fingers discover how wet I already am. My hips rock against his hand, seeking more pressure.

I reach behind me, finding Korvan's massive cock. My fingers can barely wrap around its girth. I stroke him from base to tip, feeling him stir against my back.

His size used to terrify me. Now it makes my inner walls clench with anticipation.

"Fuck," Korvan mumbles, still half-asleep.

But his body's fully alert. His hips thrust into my grip instinctively.

Thalor remains asleep, his face peaceful. I shift until my breast hovers above his mouth, then slowly lower my nipple between his parted lips.

His eyes flutter open as he automatically suckles, sleepy gaze focusing on my face with dawning awareness.

Just like that, I go from being surrounded by slumbering giants to being the center of a very awake, very aroused alien trio. Their patterns pulse brighter, synchronizing with each other and with my racing heart.

Zegran's fingers work faster against my clit, two thick digits pushing inside me while his thumb maintains maddening circles. Korvan's massive hands grip my hips, guiding my strokes on his cock. Thalor's mouth moves from one nipple to the other, teeth grazing sensitive flesh just hard enough to send sparks racing down my spine.

My orgasm builds quickly, pressure coiling tight at my core. I cry out as it crests, walls clenching around Zegran's fingers. My hand tightens reflexively around Korvan's shaft, and he groans against my shoulder, hot seed spurting across my back in glowing blue streaks.

I turn my attention to Zegran, stroking him with my free hand. His ridged cock pulses beneath my palm. His patterns flare bright as he approaches climax. He comes with a growl, marking my stomach with more glowing fluid.

Thalor takes himself in hand, working his shaft while still sucking my nipples. His tech-enhanced nodules vibrate subtly along his length. Three quick strokes and he's coming too, adding his illuminated essence to the artwork covering my skin.

We collapse, breathing hard. The glowing evidence of their pleasure sinks slowly into my skin.

"Better than an alarm clock," I murmur, nestled between Zegran and Thalor while Korvan's arm drapes across all of us.

"Your arousal patterns have changed," Thalor observes, tracing lazy patterns on my hip. "Increased frequency, intensity, and duration since our initial acquisition."

I snort. "You're making me sound like a science experiment again."

"Fascinating one," Thalor replies, unperturbed.

"The manuals say human females exist in a constant state of sexual readiness," Korvan rumbles against my back. "Always wanting."

I shake my head. "That's not how it works for us. At all. My libido was practically nonexistent on Earth. Too busy trying not to die to worry about getting laid."

Zegran's eyes narrow. "Yet you initiate mating frequently now."

"Because I feel safe with you." I surprise myself by admitting it. "Last night, when you let me cry instead of just trying to fuck away my feelings, that meant something. It made me feel... seen. Understood."

They exchange glances over my head, one of those silent Drayzok communications I can't quite interpret.

"The manuals indicate emotional displays should be redirected to physical gratification," Thalor says slowly.

"Well, we've already established that the manuals are shit." I prop myself up on one elbow. "Women aren't sex robots. We're complicated. When we feel emotionally secure, that's when we can let go physically. That's when submission feels good instead of terrifying."

Korvan's hand tightens on my hip. "So submitting to us, it's been feeling good for you?"

"Yeah." I swallow hard. "Like right now, I feel... I want..."

"Tell us," Zegran commands, his voice dropping to that register that makes my insides clench.

"I want to submit to you. All of you. Show you what it looks like when it's real. When it's chosen."

Three pairs of glowing eyes darken with hunger. Without a word, they position me on my back in the center of our sleeping platform. Thalor moves between my thighs while Zegran and Korvan pin my wrists above my head.

Thalor enters me slowly, his ridged length stretching me in the most delicious way.

I remember what he told me about Drayzok bioluminescence during sex—how the patterns can transfer between partners during moments of intense connection.

His geometric patterns pulse brighter as he thrusts, sending waves of pleasure through my nerve endings. His cock's ridges and nodules press against sensitive spots I never would've known existed before my trio.

My climax builds, pressure gathering at every point where our bodies connect. When Thalor comes, hot and pulsing inside me, my orgasm crashes through me.

Glowing blue semen drips down my thighs as we move to the bathing suite. The giant tub fills automatically with healing waters that bubble and steam.

Korvan lifts me effortlessly, positioning me on his thick shaft. His thrusts are relentless, almost painful, stretching me beyond what should be possible.

But the healing waters swirl around us, soothing the ache even as he creates it. Pain and relief, over and over, building a pleasure so intense it borders on agony. I come screaming his name, clawing at his massive shoulders as he fills me with another load of glowing seed.

Zegran carries me back to the bedroom, laying me down. When he enters me, his usual aggression is absent, replaced by slow, deep thrusts that make me feel cherished.

"We will always care for you," he murmurs against my ear as another orgasm washes through me. "Always protect you."

Then his control snaps. His pace turns punishing, claiming me with the fierce dominance I've come to crave from him. He comes with a roar, spines fully extended, patterns blazing across his skin like lightning.

I lie boneless between them, thoroughly claimed and utterly satisfied.

***

We're sprawled across the sleeping platform, my body pleasantly sore. Sweat cools on my skin as Thalor idly traces patterns on my thigh, eyes distant with some complex calculation.

Korvan chews on a protein cube he grabbed from the dispenser, while Zegran stares at the ceiling, his gaze thoughtful.

My mind drifts to their homeworld—this mysterious planet Draxith that they sometimes mention but never fully describe. On Earth, knowing your enemy gave you an edge. Here, I know these guys aren't my enemy anymore, but I still know next to nothing about where they come from.

"Tell me about Draxith," I say, breaking the comfortable silence. "What's it like there?"

They turn to me with varying degrees of surprise on their faces.

"You want to know more about our home?" Zegran asks.

"Well, yeah. I mean, I've been living with you guys for weeks, and all I know is it's far away and has weird weather."

Zegran's patterns pulse in what I've learned is thoughtfulness. "What aspect interests you?"

"Everything. What do you miss most about it?"

His eyes soften slightly, spines relaxing against his back. "The electrical storms. Great energy discharges that light up entire continents.

During peak season, the sky remains bright for days, pulsing with colors your human eyes would struggle to perceive."

He gestures to the lightning patterns on his skin. "My clan lived in the Storm Plains. We built energy collection towers taller than any structure on your Earth. Standing atop one during a convergence storm..." His voice trails off, uncharacteristically wistful.

"You'd stand in electrical storms on purpose?" I prop myself up on my elbows, fascinated.

"It strengthens our natural patterns." Zegran touches the glowing markings on his chest. "The energy feeds us, connects us to Draxith itself."

"That sounds beautiful," I say. "What about you, Thalor? What do you miss most?"

Thalor's eyes brighten. "The tech temples. Ancient structures housing the knowledge of generations. The central temple in Korda-Dren houses a neural network containing the collective technological discoveries of our species for twelve thousand years." His patterns pulse faster with excitement. "The interface allows direct communication with the stored consciousness of our greatest innovators. I spent thirty-two cycles studying there before my warrior assignment."

"You can talk to your ancestors? Like, actually talk to them?"

"Simplified explanation, but essentially correct." Thalor nods. "Their neural patterns are preserved, allowing limited interaction. Less conversation, more consulting a highly responsive database."

I turn to Korvan. "And you? What do you miss?"

Korvan grunts, cracking his neck. "The Combat Arenas." He notices my expression and elaborates grudgingly. "Natural formations in the Northern Wastes. Canyons carved by ancient floods, perfect acoustics. Fighting there, it's different than here. Purer. The sound of blade against blade echoes for miles."

"Korvan earned his warrior status there," Zegran adds. "Youngest champion in eight generations."

Korvan shrugs, clearly uncomfortable with the praise. "It was nothing. Good terrain, weak opponents."

"He defeated nineteen challengers in succession," Thalor clarifies. "Without rest or sustenance. Traditional ritual typically expected five victories at most."

"On that day, the only one prouder than Thalor and I was Korvan's brother. He nearly ripped apart another challenger for insulting Korvan's honor."

I stare at Korvan with new appreciation. "So you're basically a celebrity?"

"Was," Korvan corrects, his patterns dimming slightly. "Before everything changed."

"What changed?" I ask, sensing something important.

They exchange glances, that silent communication again.

"Our society is... unbalanced," Zegran says carefully. "Males significantly outnumber females."

"By approximately sixteen to one," Thalor adds. "Traditionally, a Drayzok female who mates with a trio of males stays with them to raise offspring."

"But there aren't enough females," I fill in.

"Worse than that," Korvan says. "Many don't even want males at all anymore."

Thalor's expression grows analytical. "Over the past several generations, there has been a significant shift among Drayzok females toward sapphic relationships. Most are now bisexual, with approximately thirty-eight percent exclusively lesbian."

"The cause is unknown," Zegran continues. "Some believe it's biological evolution, others claim it's cultural."

"Either way," Korvan says bitterly, "more males compete for fewer willing females each generation."

"So what happens to all the males who can't find mates?" I ask.

"They remain unmated," Zegran states simply. "Some join specialized military orders that forbid personal attachments. Others become obsessed with finding a mate, driving much of our competitive culture."

"And some grow... resentful," Thalor adds carefully. "A faction believes females should be forced to mate, creating significant societal division."

"In response, females have become increasingly reclusive," Zegran explains. "Many retreat to remote mountain ranges, forming female-only communities. Some never interact with males at all."

I can't help but laugh. "Honestly, if I had to deal with a bunch of angry, entitled men all day, I'd probably become a reclusive lesbian too."

Their expressions range from confused to hurt.

"You would prefer females?" Korvan asks, his deep voice uncharacteristically vulnerable.

My smile fades as I realize he's serious. "No, that's not—I was just joking. I'm very attracted to you. All of you."

"Sexual attraction patterns are complex," Thalor says, shifting back to his comfort zone of analysis. "Our males have evolved physical adaptations to enhance partner pleasure. The ridges, the bioluminescent reactions. There's a theory that these traits were developed to increase our appeal to potential mates."

"Wait, so your amazing dick is literally an evolutionary response to getting rejected?" I bite my lip to keep from laughing again.

"Unconfirmed theory," Thalor admits. "But the timing of these adaptations corresponds with the female preference shift."

I consider this new information, pieces clicking together in my mind. A species with a desperate shortage of willing mates. Males who may never find partners. An entire culture built around competition for increasingly scarce female attention.

"That's why the Original Agents' lies worked so well," I say slowly. "They told you exactly what you wanted to hear—that human women would be perfect mates. That we're submissive and exist just for sex and reproduction. That we secretly enjoy being dominated."

"The timing was fortuitous," Thalor acknowledges. "Earth's need for protection coincided with our most severe mating crisis in recorded history."

"You were vulnerable," I say, not accusingly, but with dawning understanding. "You wanted to believe them."

"It doesn't excuse what happened to you," Zegran says firmly. "Or to other human females."

"No, it doesn't," I agree. "But it helps me understand why having a mate is so important to you three."

Korvan shifts closer, his massive hand engulfing mine. "Not just any mate. For us, it's not just about mating or breeding anymore. It's about you."

"About how we feel about you," Thalor says. "And even about envisioning you as the mother of our children. If fortune favored us, we could have a lineage carrying both our blood and yours."

Carrying children for my trio? Suddenly, the thought of being bred by the Drayzok is not as horrifying as it once was.

"It's true, Quinn." Zegran's voice drops to that intensity that makes my chest tight. "This is no longer about claiming or possession. We... I love you."

I blink, sure I've misheard. "What?"

"I love you as well," Thalor says in a serious voice. "Some would say the emotion defies logical analysis, yet it persists, nonetheless."

Korvan just nods once, and then he seems to realize this is one of those times when it's worth saying the thing out loud, even if it involves feelings.

"I love you, our little mate."

My mouth opens and closes. What the hell am I supposed to say to that? The alien warriors who kidnapped me, claimed me, hunted me down when I escaped... now professing love?

And the craziest part is, I think they mean it.

Before I can come up with a response, Zegran's personal communication device chimes. His patterns flicker with surprise as he checks it.

"The Command Council," he says, exchanging glances with the others. "They request immediate contact."

They rise in unison, moving toward the communication suite in the adjacent room. The door slides shut behind them, leaving me alone with my tangled thoughts.

Love. They said they love me.

Is this my life now? Forever?

That's what it felt like to hear that. Like I'll be here, with them, forever.

But not just with them. I'd be living among the Drayzok, even with everything I know about them.

What would I even go back to on Earth? A ruined planet. Constant struggle for basic necessities. Rust Rats and raiders. Trading with people like Estelle for just enough scraps to survive another day.

Here, I have three powerful protectors who've proven they'll fight for me. Even against their own authorities. They'd make sure I'm safe, fed, cared for. They'd never abandon me.

But is that enough reason to stay? To accept a life away from my own kind, my own planet?

My own kind. Can I even say I'm the same kind as humans like the Rust Rats? The Original Agents? They sure don't treat people like me as one of their own.

The door slides open, and my trio returns. Their patterns pulse with intensity.

"What is it?" I ask, sitting up straighter.

"There will be another Command Council hearing," Zegran says.

"Why? They already rejected our petition."

"They won't tell us why," Korvan says grimly.

"We can only hope it's not a punishment tribunal," Thalor says. "For our violations."

I gulp. Punishment? Like they did to the warriors who went after me? Would the Council do that to my trio?

Would I survive if I had to witness it?

CHAPTER 28

QUINN

Cold air slaps my skin as we approach the Command Council chambers. This time is different, and not only because it's supposed to be super rare for the Council to do a second hearing after they shot down a petition.

It's different because this time, Zegran's holding onto a thin metal leash.

And at the other end of that leash? That'd be me.

Walking beside him.

Bare-ass naked.

We stride past a group of unmated warriors, and their conversation dies mid-sentence. Their patterns flare bright as they take in my tits, my legs, my belly.

One of them licks his lips. Korvan growls, stepping closer to my side like a shield.

"Eyes forward," Thalor murmurs to me, brushing his fingers across my lower back. "Remember our strategy."

Strategy. Right. That's what this little stunt is supposed to be.

"We need to show them something unexpected," Korvan had said yesterday in our quarters. "Demonstrate that human females with translator chips can still be submissive mates."

"What are you suggesting?" Zegran said.

"We bring her naked. Leashed. Let them see with their own eyes that a female can understand our language, speak her mind, and still choose to submit."

"That's insane." Thalor's patterns sparked like he was about to pop a vein. "After what we learned about Poltar and males like him? Parading Quinn naked in front of hundreds of unmated warriors could trigger a frenzy."

"Or worse," Zegran added, "reinforce their belief that human females are just objects for their pleasure."

I watched them argue, already picturing what it would feel like to be exposed in that great chamber, with all those eyes on my bare body. The fear. The vulnerability.

The power.

"I'll do it," I said, cutting into their debate.

All three heads whipped to me at once.

"Think about it," I said. "What's the Council's biggest argument against translator chips? That we'd stop being good little sex toys. So let's prove them wrong. Let's show them what happens when a human chooses to submit—not because she's scared, but because she wants to."

Korvan squeezed my hand. "Exactly."

The way they'd all looked at me then, with pride on their faces and in their light patterns, made my face go hot.

Getting ready this morning had been pretty special. They'd taken their sweet time peeling my clothes off, one piece at a time.

Zegran's hands lingered when my tits sprang free.

"So soft," he'd murmured, cupping my breast. "So perfect."

Thalor had slid my pants down, his breath hot against my thigh.

"The Council doesn't even know what they're missing. A human female who can debate tech specs one moment and surrender completely the next."

Korvan was the one to clip the leash on, placing a leathery collar snugly around my neck.

"Can't wait to drag you back here after this shitshow," he growled. "Gonna fuck you until you forget all about the Council and scream our names."

I'd been wet just from their words.

And now I'm about to walk into a whole chamber full of Drayzok men with nothing covering my skin.

Am I scared? Hell fucking yeah.

But there's something else, too. There's the fact that I'm using these men's expectations against them.

Which means that, despite how it looks like I'm at their mercy, I'm the one walking in there with power.

Nobody but my guys could get me to do something like this. Not because they can force me—though that too, if they really wanted to—but because they're the only ones who've ever truly seen me. All of me.

I can let go and let them handle me, and still know that they see me for who I fully am. They never forget my fire.

Right before the doors to the Council chamber, Zegran stops and faces me.

"Whatever happens today, I want you to know, Quinn. I'll never stop fighting for your kind. I'll change our society for you however I can. Once, I believed such change was impossible. Not anymore. Not since I've come to love you."

I blink. My eyes are warm and wet.

"I join in this vow," Thalor says. "Our ancestors' wisdom was meant to elevate, not subjugate. I will work to restore that true purpose."

Korvan gives a snort. "Same. Anyone tries to stop us, I'll rip their fucking arms off."

That rattles a laugh out of me. "Well, if I'd known all it would take to reform society was letting you three fuck me senseless, I'd have volunteered way sooner."

I let out a long breath after they each kiss me. "But seriously. Thank you for seeing us, seeing me, as worth fighting for. So many humans wouldn't do that for each other, let alone aliens."

It makes me want to stay here with them even more.

The chamber doors swing open, and all conversation inside instantly dies.

Hundreds of Drayzok men are sitting here again. And all their eyes are on my naked body.

I keep my chin up, shoulders square. Let them look. That's what I'm here for.

The wave of lust that hits the crowd is almost palpable. Patterns light up, and I can practically feel their envy for my trio.

The others wish they could hold me on a leash.

I hope they get the point. This perfect submission they all so desperately crave? I can give it to my trio only thanks to the translation chip.

Threg is here, sitting with the other Council members. So is that pig, Poltar.

We take our seats near the center, and I'm not hidden behind my trio this time. I'm on display. A message. A challenge.

And I'm ready.

The central Council member rises. I watch his robes swirl, and I'm hyper-aware of how I'm the only one naked here.

His ancient face gives away nothing as he raises a hand to begin.

"This hearing has been convened at the request of Technician Rylak of the Third Order," he announces.

Wait, what? My head snaps up so fast, my neck cracks.

Rylak? The stick-up-his-ass technician who had to be threatened into giving me a translation chip? The one who acted like I'd contaminate his precious tech with my human touch?

Zegran shifts beside me. "What does this mean?" he whispers to Thalor.

"I don't know." Thalor shakes his head. "He was adamantly opposed to Quinn having a translator chip. This could be... problematic."

"Frax," Korvan curses.

The central Council member gestures to the technicians' section.

"Technician Rylak, you may approach and speak."

The crowd murmurs as Rylak rises. The Council members visibly straighten, their postures shifting from authoritative to respectful. It's like watching kings bow to a priest.

Rylak moves to the center of the chamber. He glances at me, naked and leashed, then looks away, like he doesn't want to stare too long.

Zegran's grip on my leash goes tight.

Rylak faces the Council, performing a complex salute I've never seen before.

"Honored Council, I come before you to make a confession and share a revelation."

You could hear a pin drop.

"I am the technician who provided the translator chip to the human female Quinn Morgyn."

Gasps ripple. One Council member half-rises from his seat, outrage on his face, but the center guy motions him back down.

"I violated our most sacred protocols," Rylak continues. "I allowed warriors to coerce me into breaking the prohibition against giving human females translation technology."

He's throwing us under the bus. My stomach knots. So much for our strategy. We're fucked.

But Rylak isn't finished.

"After this transgression, I sought forgiveness in the tech temple. I communed with the ancestors for several days, seeking their wisdom." His patterns pulse brighter. "And they answered."

Even the Council members seem to hold their breaths.

"Our ancestors gifted us technology to elevate ourselves. The purpose of translation technology is to bridge gaps between species." Rylak gestures at me. "After hearing Quinn Morgyn speak at the previous hearing, after witnessing her intelligence and reason, I can no longer deny what my sacred duty demands."

Wait, is he...?

"I believe that my duty as a technician includes bridging the communication gap between Drayzok and human mates. I support the petition of these warriors. Human females should have access to translator technology."

Holy shit.

"Did he just *help* us?" I whisper.

"It appears so," Thalor murmurs back. "Technician support changes the dynamics significantly."

There's a stunned silence in the chamber, then an explosion of voices. Drayzok arguing with each other, patterns flashing in agitation. The Council members huddle together, their ancient faces pinched.

I look at Poltar, sitting rigidly in his seat, patterns so dark, they're almost black. He looks furious, but he's not saying anything. He wouldn't publicly oppose a technician.

A technician's word carries weight that even a Council member can't easily dismiss. Rylak just handed us a fucking nuclear bomb.

Hope flutters in my chest.

The central Council member finally gets everyone quiet.

"The Council acknowledges Technician Rylak's testimony. We will—"

"I wish to speak." It's Poltar.

The central member inclines his head, clearly unhappy, but letting it happen.

Poltar stands, moving to the edge of the platform. But instead of addressing the Council or the audience, he looks right at me.

"With respect to the Technician Order, I must address the real issue here. This human female's inappropriate influence on the Drayzok around her."

He drags his eyes over my naked body, but he's not just looking at me with lust. It's also hate.

"Look at her," he says. "Standing naked in this sacred chamber, manipulating our males with her flesh, using her translator chip to poison the minds of warriors and even a technician."

I can feel Zegran stiffening through the leash, his spines fully extended.

"This is not the proper place for a human female in Drayzok society," Poltar declares. "Their place is in submission, in service, in silence. Not speaking in our chambers. Not challenging our ways."

Thalor squeezes my hand, reminding me: don't react.

"I see right through this pathetic display," Poltar sneers, gesturing to my naked body and to the leash around my neck. "You think to sway us by tempting us with your body? It only proves how dangerous you are."

Whispers pass through the crowd. Some Drayzok nod, and some look unsure, glancing between Poltar and Rylak.

"These warriors have been thoroughly manipulated by their mate. Which proves exactly why giving translator chips to human females would harm our society." Poltar's voice rises. "These three warriors were once exemplary. Now they act against their own kind, challenging sacred protocols, all because of this, this..."

He switches to a Drayzok word the translator doesn't catch, but from the shocked gasps around the chamber, it must be truly vile.

Vile in any language, he adds, "This little human cunt has turned loyal warriors into traitors. And for what? So she can talk back? So she can pretend to be more than the warm hole she was designed to be?"

I hear Korvan's knuckles crack. Zegran's patterns are so bright, I can't even look at him. Thalor has gone cold and hard.

But Poltar's still not done. He steps to the very edge of the dais, looking down at me like I'm something he found stuck to his boot.

"If you wish to argue that translator chips don't disrupt proper relations between Drayzok and human females, then prove it. Be their little whore here, now, in front of all of us."

The chamber erupts. The Council members look furious, but a lot of the Drayzok look excited.

The central Council member yells for order.

Poltar looks at me with triumph in his eyes. He thinks he's got me. Either I refuse and prove his point that human females with translators won't properly submit, or I agree and degrade myself completely, proving humans are just fucktoys after all.

Either way, he wins.

What the fuck am I supposed to do now?

CHAPTER 29

QUINN

The chamber is dead silent, all eyes on me as Poltar's words echo through the vast space. My stomach drops.

Be their whore in front of everyone? Does that mean what I think it means?

I whisper to Zegran, "What exactly is he asking me to do?"

Zegran's jaw ticks. "He's challenging us to prove our claims through public demonstration."

"Public demonstration?" Are we all lightheaded, or is that just me? "You mean... here. Now?"

"Yep. He wants us to fuck you in front of everyone," Korvan says bluntly.

"Public displays of submission aren't unusual for us," Zegran explains, voice tight. "By dominating a submissive mate in front of others, we demonstrate our position in the hierarchy."

Thalor leans over. "Quinn, if you refuse, Poltar wins. Your rejection of public submission would confirm his argument that translator chips for human females would disrupt proper social order. The Council will use it as evidence to rule against us."

"In other words," I say, "if I don't let you three fuck me in front of everyone, they'll never give translator chips to other women."

"Precisely," Thalor confirms.

Korvan shifts behind me, sliding his hand to my hip.

"Can't deny I find the idea stimulating," he rumbles, his patterns brightening.

Zegran shoots him a look that could melt steel. "Is your cock all you can think about at a time like this?"

"Just being honest," Korvan grunts.

I squeeze Zegran's arm. "Hey. Don't."

They all look at me, confused.

"Don't hold back. If you're into this, I want to know. Makes me want it, too."

Their eyes widen.

"You would consider this?" Thalor asks carefully.

I look out at the chamber. At Poltar's smug, punchable face. At the crowd of Drayzok men watching to see what I'll do. I think of Katarina, of all the women who might never get a voice unless I do this.

I set my jaw. "Yeah. I'll do it. I'll submit to you guys. Right here, right now."

Thalor grips my shoulders, turning me to face him. "Quinn, be certain you understand what you're agreeing to. This means submissive sex, in public. We will fuck you hard, while all these men watch."

"I get it." My voice comes out steady. "And I'm saying yes."

Zegran studies my face, searching for doubt. Finding none, he nods once, then tugs hard on the leash.

I stumble forward as he leads me to the center of the chamber.

The crowd ripples with surprise. Even Poltar's smug expression slips for a second. He didn't think I'd step up.

Tough shit, asshole.

My bare skin prickles with goosebumps as we reach the open area directly in front of the Council's elevated platform. I feel every eye in the room on my naked body. They're on my breasts, my belly, my ass, and the patch of hair between my thighs.

This is fucking insane by human standards. It's like having sex in the middle of a congressional hearing while C-SPAN broadcasts it live.

But for the Drayzok, this is about their all-mighty dominance. And right now, it's about proving that a human woman with a translation chip can still choose to submit.

The men watching us shift restlessly. Some lean forward in their seats, patterns brightening with undisguised lust. Others whisper to each other, pointing at my curves.

The air's thick with wanting. I know it'll only get thicker when the fucking starts.

My face burns with the humiliation of being pushed into this position. But there's also something darkly exciting about being the center of attention, about knowing I'm the one they want.

They can look, but they can't touch.

Only my trio gets to touch.

Zegran yanks the leash, pulling me down to my knees. He leans down to me.

"Are you certain about this?" he whispers.

I lift my head, meeting his eyes. "I'm sure. I trust you. All of you. Give it your all. Don't hold back."

His eyes flash, like he's sort of amazed, and definitely proud. He nods once, then stands.

Then he shoves me forward onto all fours.

The sudden movement draws a collective intake of breath from the crowd.

"Stay down," Zegran commands, his voice no longer a whisper, but a growl meant for everyone to hear.

I'm on my hands and knees, ass up. My breasts hang heavy beneath me, nipples tightening in anticipation. I've never felt so exposed, so utterly on display.

Zegran's hand cracks down on my ass. The sharp sting makes me whimper. Another smack follows, harder this time, then another and another until my flesh burns.

Korvan and Thalor join in, and the collective impact is so hard, it rocks me forward. My soft flesh jiggles and bounces, drawing appreciative growls from the watching crowd.

It hurts. It's humiliating. But my body loves it, thighs shaking, pussy clenching.

Korvan grabs my hips, roughly turning me so my ass faces the crowd.

"Look!" he shouts, his deep voice carrying through the chamber. "See how she takes our discipline? See how her flesh marks for us?"

I should be dying of shame. Instead, I feel a perverse pride.

"Spread her," Zegran commands. "Show them what belongs to us. Let them see how she drips for her masters."

Korvan pries my ass cheeks apart, putting my holes on display. The stares feel hungry.

"Look at our little whore," Korvan says. "Spread open for all to see. You can watch her holes, but you'll always know they belong to us."

My face burns hotter.

I'm not prepared when Korvan brings his hand down hard between my legs, slapping his thick fingers directly on my clit.

I scream, hearing my own voice bouncing off the chamber walls and crying back at me. The pain is sharp, a jolt of forbidden pleasure. Fluid drips from my slit.

And Korvan makes sure everyone sees.

"See how wet she gets?" he shouts. "Look how she responds to discipline! Look how she craves it!"

I catch Poltar's eye and hold his gaze, refusing to look away even as Korvan continues to display me. I give him the coldest, hardest stare I can manage.

You thought I'd break, didn't you? You thought I'd refuse, or cry, or beg for mercy.

Wrong.

When another slap lands on my ass, I moan loudly, making sure every Drayzok in the chamber can hear my pleasure.

"Yes! Please, more! I need it!"

Poltar looks like he swallowed a bug. Good.

"I'm yours!" I shout, looking from Zegran to Thalor to Korvan. "Your little whore. I give myself to you. Use me!"

My words ring through the chamber. I see the surprise on the faces of the Council members, the shock rippling through the crowd. This is what they didn't see coming. A human woman with a voice, on all fours, begging for it.

I've never felt more powerful.

Thalor steps in front of me, his cock level with my face. It's jutting straight out, the geometric patterns along its length pulsing with bright light.

He cups my chin, tilting my face up to meet his gaze.

"Ready?"

I nod, opening my mouth to take him in. He brings his cock to my lips.

And that's when I realize he wasn't just asking if I'm ready to suck him off.

At the exact moment when Thalor pushes his cock between my lips, Zegran rams into my pussy from behind.

Before I can even process that double invasion, Korvan spreads my ass cheeks wide, and begins forcing his cock—the biggest of the three—into my tightest hole.

Oh, fuck.

It's the way they all push in at once that gets to me.

My scream of surprise is muffled by Thalor's cock filling my mouth, pushing deeper until he cuts off my breath. Zegran's ridged cock forces my pussy open, giving me no time to adjust. And Korvan—sweet gods—his cock feels like it's splitting me in half as it forces its way into my ass.

My body shudders between them, stretched to the limit.

"Look at her taking all of us at once," Zegran growls to the crowd, gripping my hips. "A perfect mate."

I hear slapping sounds. Are the Drayzok around us jerking off? With my eyes full of tears, I can't see them to know for sure.

I choke around Thalor's length, and it's my only chance to catch my breath. He keeps pushing forward, hitting the back of my throat.

Korvan finally eases up a little, pulling partway out from my ass. But he does that only to drive into me again, even harder this time.

Zegran's lightning patterns flash bright as he pounds into my pussy. His ridges grind on my clit. The suction they create pulls at my most sensitive spots, making me clench and spasm.

I'm so full, stuffed by all of them, just holes for them to use.

And everyone is watching.

My tears finally fall, clearing my blurry vision.

The crowd is hypnotized. Drayzok cocks are out, jerking furiously. Some men are standing, some barely hanging onto the edge of their seats. Some grip their armrests so hard, I can see the metal bending.

Even the Command Council members lean forward on their elevated platform, faces twisted with undisguised lust.

The central member's robes are tented, his hand disappearing beneath the fabric. The guy next to him isn't even pretending to hold back. He has his cock out, stroking it openly as he watches us.

Power surges through me. I'm on my knees, stuffed with alien cock, being used like a common whore.

And yet, I'm the one powerful enough to make these men lose control.

Poltar's face has shock all over it. He didn't think I could do this. And not only am I doing it, I'm embracing it.

The trio slows their pace, adjusting positions and giving me a second to breathe. Thalor withdraws from my mouth, a string of saliva connecting us as he studies my face.

"Good?" he asks quietly, just for me. Zegran goes slower, in deep. Korvan rubs small circles on my lower back.

I nod, unable to form words.

Behind the brutal display, I feel their care. The crowd can't tell, but I know it's there. Zegran's angling his thrusts to hit the spot that makes me feel good. Thalor's gauging my breathing, letting me choke enough to put on a show, but still catch my breath. Korvan's supporting my weight, taking the strain off my trembling limbs.

They're giving the audience the show they expect, but they're thinking of me.

I know how it goes. I'm also giving them something because I care. This is far outside of the comfort zone of human behavior, but I'm showing my respect for their ways.

Funny how I used to swear I'd rather die than let a Drayzok touch me. In my mind, they were all monsters.

Now I'm on my hands and knees before hundreds of them, being fucked by three at once, and doing it willingly.

Not because I've been broken. Not because I've given up. But because I know I'm worth fighting for. All those other women like me are worth taking a chance for, and making a change for.

I submit because I'm stronger now.

I moan, getting closer to that blissful state where I just take the fucking, because I can't do anything but feel. My warriors rock me between them, their skin glowing with pleasure.

Then something strange happens.

A warmth tingles over my body, kind of like I feel when my trio ejaculates on me. Only nobody's climaxed yet.

"Look!" someone shouts from the crowd. "Her skin!"

Other Drayzok gasp. Behind me, Korvan and Zegran stop moving. Thalor pulls out of my mouth, his eyes wide as he stares at my body.

"What?" I pant, looking down at myself. "What is it?"

Now it's my turn to gasp.

My skin is glowing. Actually glowing, with faint blue patterns that mirror the ones on my trio's bodies.

Zegran's lightning bolts trace down my arms and back. Thalor's geometric shapes shimmer across my breasts. Korvan's swirls circle my thighs.

"Khal'ven," Thalor breathes, the word filled with wonder.

"What does that mean?" My voice is hoarse from his cock.

His patterns pulse faster as he explains. "During Drayzok matings, mates who care deeply for one another can start reflecting each other's patterns. It's called khal'ven." His fingers trace the glowing marks on my skin. "We consider it sacred. It's never been observed in a human before."

I blink. "So... the fact that it's happening now..."

"It means you're truly bonded to us." Thalor's voice is thick with emotion. "And it suggests that human females are far more compatible with Drayzok than anyone believed."

"It means we're fucking winning," Korvan adds with a roar. He starts up again, slamming into my ass with a triumphant thrust.

Zegran whoops and joins him, thrusting into my pussy.

Thalor laughs as he shoves his cock back in my mouth, fucking my throat with renewed urgency.

I surrender to it, letting them use me, giving myself completely to this moment.

Thalor comes first, his hot seed flooding my mouth, spilling down my chin when I can't swallow fast enough. The metallic-sweet taste fills my senses as he pulls out, painting more glowing streaks across my face and breasts.

Zegran and Korvan aren't far behind. They come together, rocking their cocks inside me, filling my pussy and ass with their hot, glowing cum.

That does me in. The sensation of being filled from both ends triggers my own orgasm. It's a blinding explosion that tears through me, making me scream.

My body convulses between them, milking their cocks for every drop of their glowing seed.

They withdraw only to mark me further, Zegran painting my back while Korvan covers my ass and thighs with pulsing streaks. They rub it into my skin, stopping to admire how it mixes with my new light patterns.

Finally, they lift me between them, my limp body supported by their massive arms. They roar in unison, a primal sound of victory.

The crowd loses it. Warriors howl and beat the benches. The air is thick with the scent of semen.

When the room finally quiets, my trio carries me back to our seats. I'm sticky with sweat and cum, holes throbbing, skin still glowing.

I hold my head high.

My legs barely support me, so Zegran holds me across his lap while we wait. The Council members huddle together, talking in low, heated voices.

Thalor takes my hand. Korvan claims the other.

Yep, I once swore I'd never let a Drayzok touch me. Now my three are touching me, and it's the most comforting feeling I've ever known.

All because I trust my guys. Can't believe my trust in them might help save my kind.

The central Council member rises. The chamber falls silent.

"After consideration of the evidence presented, including the unprecedented khal'ven manifestation in a human female, the Council has reached a decision."

I hold my breath.

"Translator chips will be made available to human female mates on a case-by-case basis, beginning immediately."

My heart leaps. Poltar looks like he wants to puke.

"Furthermore," the Council member continues, "all operations with the Earth gang known as the Rust Rats will be suspended, pending investigation into their mate acquisition practices."

I'm probably supposed to keep quiet, but I can't help myself. I let out a loud yelp, pumping my fist into the air.

Zegran could punish me for it, but he just laughs, tightening his arms around me. Thalor and Korvan squeeze my hands and kiss my head.

We did it. It's not a complete victory, but it's enough to start changing things. Enough to give women like Katarina a chance.

The closing bell rings out over the chamber.

Zegran lifts me from his lap, spinning me in a circle before crushing his mouth to mine in a bruising kiss.

When he finally releases me, Thalor takes me in his arms and kisses me, grinning against my mouth.

Korvan practically yanks me from Thalor's arms, crushing me against his chest and claiming my mouth until I can't breathe.

Winning with my guys. It's the best feeling in the universe.

CHAPTER 30

QUINN

The liquor tastes like fire and acid. It's heavy, full of some greatly treasured Drayzok metal that gleams blue-black.

All my respect to the Drayzok for being able to handle it. But as for me, I can't say I'm sorry to pass it off when Zegran takes the ceremonial chalice from me.

It's gonna be my turn again before I know it, and I'll take my gulp like a champ, but I'm gonna try my damndest to forget it exists until then.

The guys told me this is tradition after a win: pass the single cup. Take turns drinking until you either pass out or, if you're mates, fuck each other senseless.

So far, we're still in the drinking phase, but judging by the way Korvan's patterns pulse brighter with each sip and how Thalor keeps "accidentally" brushing against my thigh, we're heading rapidly toward option two.

I stare at my arm, because my light patterns are getting more fascinating with every gulp I take. They've faded since the Council hearing, but I can still see the faint blue lines, like ghost tattoos.

Khal'ven, they call it. The sacred bond that supposedly never happens with humans.

Until me.

"Still glowing," Zegran says, tracking my gaze.

He brings his hand to my arm, running his fingertips over the patterns.

"It's unreal." I twist my wrist, watching how the faint blue shimmers. "All of it."

Not just the light show raving under my skin, but everything. Beating Poltar. Getting translator chips for human women. Shutting down the Rust Rats' sleazy operation.

Just a few months ago, I was hiding out from them in burned-out buildings. Now I wanna find them and gloat in their faces about taking them down.

That was me, fuckwipes.

Korvan grabs the chalice, drains the rest in one go, and wipes his mouth.

Whew. I'm off the hook.

"Your territory will be safer now," he says.

Yeah, no kidding. If by "territory," he means the condition of my liver if I keep drinking that stuff.

"No more Rust Rats trading women," he finishes.

Oh, yeah. That.

"For now." I can't help the skepticism. "But there are still plenty of desperate assholes who'd happily sell out their own species for whatever your people are offering."

Thalor takes the chalice from Korvan and refills it. Damn!

"True," he says, "but cutting off the largest trafficking operation will create a significant deterrent effect. Other groups will see that the arrangement is no longer profitable or protected."

"And women will be safer," Zegran adds, settling beside me. "They can choose to mate with Drayzok rather than being captured."

I snort. "Yeah, but after all the threats of being kidnapped and forced into it, I'm not sure how many will line up to volunteer."

"You would," Korvan points out. "Knowing what you know now."

"Sure, now..."

"And you stayed with us." Korvan grins, showing those too-sharp teeth that used to make me tremble. "Maybe it's easier to convince women than you think."

"Yeah, like any of this was easy!" I grab the nearest pillow and chuck it at his head.

He catches it effortlessly, dark eyes gleaming with amusement.

"It's gonna take time," I tell them. "To undo the damage, to build trust. Women from Earth have every reason to fear the Drayzok."

Thalor sips from the chalice, his patterns pulsing thoughtfully. "You are troubled. Are you not pleased with our victory?"

I sigh, slumping back against the cushions. "Of course I am. It's just..."

"What's on your mind?" Thalor passes the chalice to Zegran, then shifts closer to me.

"This was just one battle. A small one." I trace the fading patterns on my arm. "We convinced, what, five Council members? On one ship? Meanwhile, there are who knows how many more Drayzok who think like Poltar. Drayzok who want their women terrified and broken."

"Not all Drayzok are like Poltar." Zegran's spines flare slightly. "Many will embrace change once we make them understand."

"And until they do? What's happening to them?" Will Katarina even get a translator chip? I can't be sure. "Poltar said there are women being shipped to Draxith right now. Two months in space with Drayzok who think they're just animals meant to be broken."

They go quiet. The ceremonial chalice stops its circuit around our circle.

"We won a battle," Thalor says. "Not yet the war."

Zegran nods. "The broader Command Council on Draxith will require more substantial evidence and lobbying to change their approach. Our victory here is significant, but it's just the start."

Korvan growls, his patterns darkening. "We'll fight them all if we have to. Change everything."

"How?" I ask. "We're just four people."

"We'll find others who think like us," Zegran says. "There are more among the Drayzok, particularly in the technician class. Rylak's intervention proved that."

"We'll need to connect, create networks," Thalor adds. "We'll work together. The evidence of khal'ven in a human female will be powerful persuasion."

"And what about the women suffering now?" I ask. "While we're building these networks?"

"We help them where we can," Zegran says. "Starting with finding your friend Katarina."

My heart squeezes. "You'd do that?"

"We'll try." He puts his hand over mine. "No guarantees, but we can access the acquisition records. If she's on this station, we'll find her."

I stare at him. He once terrified me. Now, he risks his position in his world, the position that once meant everything to him, to help women he's never even met.

Because I asked. Because it matters to me.

"Thank you," I whisper.

Zegran nods once, then lifts the chalice to his lips. I look past him to see Korvan hunched at the edge of our sleeping platform, patterns barely glowing.

I nudge his thigh with my foot. "What's with the gloomy lights?"

He doesn't look at me. "Nothing."

"Liar. You look like someone stole your favorite knife."

He cracks his neck. "I'm wondering."

"About?"

"If you'd rather go back. To Earth." He shrugs, hunching even more. "Your home is safer now. You could return."

Home. I could go back, I guess. To the ruins, the scavenging, the endless fear. Never knowing if I'd make it another day.

But I look at these three. My captors. Now, my mates. And from here forward, my... family.

Their seed could already be quickening inside me, forming a child. The thought of being bred by the Drayzok doesn't scare the shit out of me anymore, because now, it's about building my family with my trio.

"Earth isn't home anymore," I say. "This is. You three are."

Korvan's patterns light up like a sunrise. "You're staying with us?"

"I'm staying." I press in close, nestling against his side. "I want to help other women who've been captured. And I want to be with you three." I swallow hard. "I love you. All of you."

Zegran's spines go straight up. I turn to him.

"Zegran, I love you." I touch his face, feeling the slight metallic warmth of his skin. "Your strength, your leadership, the way you let your walls down for me."

His eyes lock with mine, intense and burning. "I love you, Quinn."

I turn to Thalor. "I love you, Thalor. Your mind, your curiosity, the way you question everything."

His patterns pulse brighter. "And I love you. The emotion is strong enough to defy even scientific explanation."

Finally, I face Korvan. "I love you, Korvan. Your bluntness, your protectiveness, even your grumpy moods."

A slow grin spreads across his face. "Love you too, little human."

He hauls me into his arms. Over his shoulder, I see Zegran and Thalor watching us, their patterns synchronized in pleasure.

"This is good," Korvan rumbles against my hair. "No more escaping. Too much trouble hunting you down."

I burst out laughing, and they all join in.

"Sure hope this doesn't mean you won't be throwing me around anymore." I wiggle my hips into Korvan's obvious hard-on. "Because that would be a real shame."

Zegran's eyes darken, his spines extending. "There will be plenty of that, little mate. Count on it."

"Good," I purr. "Because I plan to keep fighting you."

"We expect nothing less," Thalor says, squeezing my thigh.

They surround me now, doing that looming thing that makes me feel small. By human standards, they look terrifying—muscular bodies, sharp teeth, pulsing light patterns.

But I'm not afraid anymore.

No, that's not quite right. More like, I trust them to handle me, even when it's terrifying.

I reach for them with greedy hands, finding blue skin, ridged muscle, and hard cocks.

Zegran crushes his mouth to mine and holds it there while Thalor lifts me, setting me down on the sleeping platform. Korvan strips me down.

I'm naked beneath them, skin pulsing brighter as they grab at me.

"You are ours," Zegran growls before he finds my nipple with his mouth.

"All of you." Thalor slides his clever fingers inside me.

"Forever," Korvan adds, cock pressing against my thigh.

I arch into their touch, surrendering in my submission.

"Yours," I agree, breathless.

They feel joyful as they take turns fucking me. Zegran fills me first, deep and hard. Thalor clutches my shoulders, then takes Zegran's place, swallowing my moans into his mouth as he joins his body with mine. When he's finished, Korvan fucks me with abandon. My light patterns flare wild and hot, pulsing with his.

"Love you so much," I moan, speaking to all of them as another orgasm rolls through me.

They roar their love for me when they erupt in my pussy and on my skin.

After, they cushion me between them as we drift off to sleep. The blue patterns under my skin pulse in time with theirs.

Soon, we'll begin the real work: finding Katarina, building alliances, fighting the screwed-up parts of this whole society. It won't be easy.

But tonight, my only fight is with sleep. For as long as my eyelids will let me, I keep gazing at my fiercely loving alien warriors.

BOOK 2, ALIEN WARRIORS' PRIZE

I was supposed to be invisible.
But brutal aliens dragged me into the light.

Yep, it's me, Katarina from the trading post. One day I was keeping my head down, and the next, I was stripped on the Drayzok space station.

Command Council thinks I know secrets—secrets that could topple their grip on Earth. To them, I'm not a person. Just a subject to be tied up and interrogated.

The brutes assigned to interrogate me? They're a triad of enforcers. Their mission is to wring the truth out of me.

And they're all too happy to use their cruel tools on my curvy body.

They're igniting a fierce defiance I never knew was burning inside me. The more they push, the harder I push back. And the more I resist, the more the line between duty and desire blurs.

Will I give in to the fire they've awakened in me?
Or will these ruthless enforcers risk it all to claim me as their prize?

ALSO IN THE DRAYZOK UNIVERSE

Hunted by Alien Monsters, the series

Six women make a daring escape from the Drayzok—only to be hunted by alien predators at the height of their mating season.

Chasing Her for Pleasure
Hunting His Mate
Claiming Her First Time
Taking What's His
Bound as His Prey
Ravaging His Mate

FREE BOOK

Thanks for reading! Want more Drayzok?

Get the FREE prequel to this series, *Conquering Her Curves,* when you
sign up for my newsletter here:
www.mpirepress.com/mqrush